The Sniff Stories

When Sniff came into sight, just past the cheese counter, he started jumping over the trolleys that were lined up at the checkout counters. He was like a great hairy horse clearing the last four fences at The Grand National. As he approached the last trolley, he was tiring just slightly. Up he went at a gallop, his tongue streaming out like a rasher of bacon. It was a brave effort, but his big forefeet clipped the trolley on the side and with a great spurt of shopping, sent it smashing sideways . . .

MARYBANK P. SCHOOL
No.

The Sniff Stories

Ian Whybrow

Illustrated by
Toni Goffe

RED FOX

A Red Fox Book
Published by Arrow Books Limited
20 Vauxhall Bridge Road, London SW1V 2SA
An imprint of the Random Century Group

London Melbourne Sydney Auckland
Johannesburg and agencies throughout the world

First published by The Bodley Head 1989

Red Fox Edition 1990

Reprinted 1990

Set in Plantin
Typeset by JH Graphics Ltd, Reading

Printed and bound in Great Britain by
The Guernsey Press Co Ltd
Guernsey, C.I.

ISBN 0 09 975406

Contents

For Ann, Suzannah and Lucy,
and with special thanks to
Jennifer Hattersley.

Enter Sniff

I was quite surprised when the phone rang because I had just unscrewed the mouthpiece to have a look at what was inside. I thought I'd better find out before we went digital.

'I'll get it,' my mum said from the kitchen. She came into the room reading a book so she paid no attention to me or to the phone. When she picked it up, the mouthpiece rolled behind a pile of old *Which?* magazines and the little silver disc inside dangled down on its wires.

'Get whatever that is, Ben,' she said vaguely, through the piece of toast she had between her teeth.

'Is that you, Joanna?' shrieked the telephone.

My mother placed the receiver at a safe distance from her ear and marked her page with the piece of toast. I recognized that shriek. It belonged to Aunt Cress.

'Could you keep an eye on Sal, dear?' said my Mum to me. 'She might get on the table again.'

'Could I what?' yelled the phone.

'Not you, Cress dear,' said Mum into the phone. And then to me, 'Will you, *please*, Ben?'

I said OK, but I was interested in an article that I'd come across in one of the magazines. According to *Which?* it was 'worth thinking about' an Olympus OM2SP, a multi-mode camera with programmed exposure option and through-the-lens flash facility.

It was true. An Olympus OM2SP *was* worth thinking about, and I *was* – when I heard the sound of breaking marmalade jars and cups and saucers, and the unmistakable yell of my two-and-a-half-year-old sister Sal as she fell off the table in the kitchen. Even so, I had also heard enough of my mother's conversation with Aunt Cress to know that we could expect a visit. And a visit from Aunt Cress always meant that we were going to get *organized*.

*

When Dad got the news about Aunt Cress coming, he looked a bit worried. He looked even more worried when Mum pointed out how much tidying up there was to do, and he suddenly remembered something urgent that needed doing in the garage and disappeared. Then, when Mum started getting out the Hoover and dusters and stuff, I decided that he could probably use a bit of help. I sneaked out of the back door, pulling it quietly shut behind me, and tiptoed quickly round the side of the house. I found Dad behind the raised bonnet of the car. He was up to his elbows in the engine and deep in thought.

'But what's she coming *for*, Dad?' I asked him. 'Mum won't say. She's just gone all moody and started cleaning everything up.'

'Who, Aunt Cress?' he asked absently. He brought his hand up quickly to stop his glasses slipping off his nose and streaked it with oil as he did so. 'She says she's coming to give your mother a break.'

'A break from what?'

'Not sure,' he said, taking out his handkerchief and wiping his hands on it. He peered open-mouthed into the depths of the engine, shifting round to the side of the car to get another angle on it. He likes looking into things, my dad. He hooked his finger under the fan belt and gave it a twang. Then he suddenly dropped on one knee and squinted very intensely at something.

'Ben, old son, can you get your arm down in there?' he said, pointing to a spot under the radiator. 'I've dropped my spanner.'

Now, this is just the sort of challenge I like, but I suppose I should really have rolled my sleeves up first. Getting oil all over a clean shirt was the last straw as far as Mum was concerned. Still, if I *had* rolled my sleeves up, Mum wouldn't have done her nut at me and I wouldn't have been forced to take Sal to the kiddies' playground. And then we should never have met Sniff.

*

When Sal and I reached the playground, the second thing we did was to have an ice-cream. This was because the first thing we did was to have a go on the see-saw. I thought at first that I was sitting on a rivet or something but I felt in the back pocket of my jeans and there it was, a nice fat little pound coin. Wicked! We had a 99 with sprinkle-spronkle, nuts and strawberry syrup. It was only when I was wiping my hands on my jeans and having a good lick round my mouth that I remembered something. Mum had given me the pound to replace the jar of marmalade that Sal had knocked off the kitchen table. Ah well, it was too late by then. Pity though, after the oily shirt and the telephone *and* Aunt Cress . . . because something told me Mum and Dad weren't exactly over the moon about her visit and I knew word for word what Mum would say about me spending the marmalade money. I had the feeling that things at home could get slightly out of control.

What worried me most was Aunt Cress. If she was going to be around for a week or so, life was going to be rough. Aunt Cress is married to Uncle John, but we hardly ever see him because he does something dead important in the Army, though nobody's ever bothered to explain what. ('Sunday lunch? Jolly good. No, wait. Sorry, can't be done. Bit pressed, actually. Duty calls. But Cress'll be there. She never says no to a feed . . .' That's Uncle John.) They haven't got any children and according to my dad, they're not cut out for it.

I'm not quite sure what Aunt Cress *is* cut out for, but I think it's probably something to do with rubber gloves and bleach. Whenever she comes to our house, about two minutes after she's taken off her scarf and mac, she asks for a pinny and a bowl. She brings her own rubber gloves and bleach and off she goes, whacking bleachy water in the sinks and down the loo and along the skirting-boards and on the door handles and all over every surface that she can slosh a cloth on. It's no good trying to have a conversation with her. She doesn't talk, she shouts. And she never speaks directly to me and Sal except to warn us of the dangers of touching, drinking or standing too close to bleach. So, whenever Aunt Cress comes, we have to put up with this awful pong and the threat of instant distintegration or poisoning or whatever, and worse than that, I get lumbered with Sal and elbowed out of the house.

Sal was in a very bad mood, and Aunt Cress hadn't even arrived. She had been *difficult* ever since she fell off the table. It wasn't so much that she'd hurt herself. What niggled her was that my mum stopped her eating the marmalade off the floor in case there were any bits of broken glass in it. All the way to the park, she'd screamed and kicked up and down in her pushchair. Even when I sat her on the see-saw and bounced her up and down until her head went wobbly, she still didn't shut up completely . . . and that usually did the trick. The ice-cream worked a *bit*. It was like stuffing a sock up the end of a trumpet; the sounds that came out turned into sort of muffled honks. But as soon as she'd finished the 99, she started screaming again.

I thought the best thing would be to take her over to the sandpit for a while, which was all right while it lasted, but then she got sand in her eye and that started her off *again*, even louder. Come to think of it, most people who cover themselves all over with ice-cream and then go and muck about in a sandpit will probably get a certain amount of it in their eyes – but Sal's one of those little kids who'll do anything if it gives her an excuse to scream. Like this time, she was well upset. She scooped up two fistfuls of sand, and whanged it at me so that some of it came hissing down on to the grass where I was and the rest drifted on to the other kids who where playing in the sand-pit. When they started to yell, Sal obviously felt a lot better because she squatted down, sprang up like a jack-in-the-box and sprayed some more into the air.

By the time the mothers of Sal's howling little

victims had realized what was happening and come galloping over to the rescue, Sal had forgotten the sand in her own eye and was really enjoying herself. I'm pretty sure one of the mothers said something nasty about us, but I couldn't really hear her properly because Sal's laugh was deafening. One or two of the grown-ups round by the sandpit started forming little defensive huddles, calling their children to them, taking quick, meaningful glances in our direction. And one or two of the firmer ones were looking as though they might have to interfere. If news of this spot of bother got home today, after the other disasters, I was *dead*.

I can't tell you exactly what happened next. It was all too sudden and blurry. I heard voices, I know that. A lot of people went 'Ahhh!' as they breathed in, like the audience in a cinema watching a scary bit. Then all at once, there was this loud panting and a great pounding of paws and it was as if all the sand in the sandpit was being whipped up by some wild sort of tornado. It was brilliant. Next thing I knew, Sal was flat on her back getting licked all over by the craziest-looking dog you ever saw! As I watched, he put his great wet nose under her chin, gave a huge sniff and then this really long lick. He had a tongue like a wallpaperer's paste-brush. The next moment, he remembered an itch where his collar should have been, sat down and scratched away at it like a madman beating a rug. When that didn't work, he rolled over on his back instead and thrashed about in the sand. Finally he stood up and shook himself, sending out a storm almost as thick as the whirlwind he'd raised when he arrived.

And then it clicked . . . where his collar *should* have been! He wasn't wearing a collar. I looked all round to see where the dog's owner was, but no one at all looked as though they belonged to him.

By this time, the bystanders had shaken themselves out of their shocked state, and now that Sal was in danger, they forgot about her chucking sand about. A stern-looking lady put her own small child in the arms of a friend and marched to the edge of the sandpit. She stood in the sand near the dog and pointed like a referee sending him off.

'Off you go! Out of it! Go away, you filthy beast!' she said. 'Leave the little girl alone.' She looked at Sal doubtfully. 'Don't worry, dear. He won't hurt you.'

When the lady stuck her arm out and pointed, it had a very strange effect on the dog. He jumped up at the lady, banged his head on the underside of her arm, did a somersault and fell on his back. Then he did the same thing about ten times, yipping away as though he had his tail caught in a door. When the lady had recovered sufficiently from her astonishment, she looked down and saw that her skirt was covered with sandy paw prints.

Everyone in the playground was standing up to look, and the dog must have suddenly felt a bit shy, because he turned round three times and did a poo-poo.

I was worried for a minute that the lady might die of shock. Her face went sort of purple, like an unwashed grape. She looked at the dog and at the poo-poo as if they were a couple of unexploded bombs, grabbed Sal and me by the arms and began to march us away. She obviously thought it was only a matter of time before the germs jumped up and zapped us all.

Sal did what she always does when she gets grabbed by the arm. She went limp and sat down and that slowed the lady up enough for me to get in my emergency line. 'We're not allowed to talk to strangers,' I said loudly. That did it, of course. The lady let go immediately, blushed purple again and looked sheepishly around for support among the rest of the mothers, but none of them quite knew what to do because they had *all* told their children never to go with strangers.

'Don't worry about us, though. We're all right,' I said, doing my best to impress them with a brave little smile. 'We're going home now.'

I dumped Sal into her pushchair and began to wheel her towards the gate. I was trying to look cool and to hurry at the same time. Sal put out her fat arm and the dog scrambled out of the sandpit, lolloped over and licked her hand. Sal grabbed him by the hair on the back of his head, and he trotted happily along beside her with his tongue hanging out and dripping on to the pavement. Every now and then, he looked at her lovingly and gave her a quick sniff and a lick.

When we got to the corner of our street, we passed Miss Morris, our next-door neighbour, who was on her way to give somebody some advice, by the look of it.

'I dot a doggie,' said Sal.

'How nice,' said Miss Morris, her staring eyes bulging out more than they usually did. She hurried on, giving them both plenty of room to get by.

★

Dad was hoovering the hall when we got home. This was a sure sign that Aunt Cress really was coming to stay.

'Look what I dot,' Sal yelled above the noise of the machine. The dog tugged itself out of her clasp and attacked the Hoover, pushing at the brush with his front paws together and biting energetically at the bag. When Dad turned the machine off (which he did with great speed) the dog lay and looked at it hopefully, waiting for it to roar again.

'What is *that*?' he said.

'Dat a doggie. My doggie,' said Sal. 'He call Miff.'

By now Mum had arrived. The dog jumped up and pushed its wet nose into her apron.

'He like you. He miffing,' explained Sal.

'He certainly is,' said Mum. She didn't really know whether to be embarrassed at the amount of sniffing going on or to be pleased by the affection she was getting.

'He go *miff! miff!*' said Sal. 'Dat his name, Miff.'

'*Is* his name Sniff?' my dad asked me.

'I don't know,' I said. 'We found him in the park.'

'It is Miff,' said Sal. 'He telled me.'

'Oh, he telled you, did he?' said Mum. 'Did he by any chance tell you where he lives?'

'Yes,' said Sal. 'He live wid me.'

*

So that was how Sniff came to be part of the Moore family. We went together back to the kiddies' playground (where he did another whopper, so that Dad had to go home for a bucket and spade to clear it up) but no one there knew him.

We went to the police station and the Sergeant said that no one had rung in to say that they'd lost him. My Dad said he wasn't surprised and the Sergeant said that somebody was probably missing him badly. He changed his mind when Sniff sicked up some sand in the waiting-room and I think he was pleased when Mum agreed to take him home and look after him until somebody claimed him.

So far, nobody has.

Oh, I forgot about Aunt Cress. She was supposed to arrive at two o'clock in the afternoon. The doorbell rang at fifteen seconds past two. Mum opened the door and Aunt Cress stood on the doorstep with her enormous suitcase.

'Darlings! Hope I'm not late!' she shouted, closing her eyes and pushing her lips into the kissing position which meant that somebody was supposed to kiss her. Mum did, and then Dad, who took the suitcase.

Sal was held up to kiss her but turned away at the moment of contact so that she bonked Aunt Cress on the eyebrow with the back of her head.

'Shouldn't be surprised if I *am* late. Blasted traffic . . . Don't I get a kiss from Ben?' she said to a coathook as she whipped off her mac and scarf. I stepped forward bravely but she yelled at Mum, 'The awkward age, eh? Ah well, we were the same as nippers, weren't we, Joanna? No time for nonsense. Now how are you, old gel? Looking a bit peaky, a bit under the weather. Overdoing it, I expect. Never mind, I shall soon have you *organized*. Good *grief*! What on earth is *that*?'

Mum and Dad had planned to give Aunt Cress time to get used to the idea of Sniff, but Sal had got the back door open and here he was. Within two seconds, he had laddered Aunt Cress's tights, pinned her against the coats and licked off one of her false eyelashes.

By supper time, the house was unrecognizably tidy and smelled like a hospital. That was only to be expected – but for someone famous throughout the known universe for her hearty appetite, Aunt Cress didn't seem all that hungry. What I mean is, she was hungry to start with. She tucked into her leek and potato soup quite happily, making little smacking noises with her lips – until she found a long sandy hair in it. Then she went rather quiet, put her spoon down and didn't eat anything else. She didn't seem to be able to take her eyes off Sniff who sat faithfully beside Sal, diving for bits of food and giving her spoon a lick whenever she let it dangle down.

Later I heard her booming away to Mum in the kitchen about *Hygiene*. And although she had brought her suitcase, she suddenly remembered something so important that it couldn't wait until the morning and she put her suitcase back in the car and drove off home.

It's a funny thing. My Dad is not all that fond of animals, but just before I went to bed that night, I went into the sitting-room to say goodnight and I saw him giving Sniff a really friendly pat.

Sniff, Miss Morris and a Bit of Cuckoo Spit

I don't think my sister Sal would have bitten my finger quite so hard if I hadn't tried to get the worm out of her mouth. Normally I wouldn't have bothered but this was one of *mine*. I had collected a number of them in a shoebox which I had carefully *placed* (not left lying around) near the lettuces by the back fence in the garden. I knew it was one of mine because it was encased in a particularly rich black mud that I had created to give them the sense that they were on holiday, rather than the subjects of a scientific investigation. I had had one or two tips from Miss Salt in Biology about how hermaphrodites breed, but I wanted to see for myself how things worked out when you put them together.

'Dop it!' screamed Sal, kicking out as I tried to lever her mouth open with my finger and thumb.

'Give it to me!' I said firmly. 'You eat your own.'

'I found it!' she insisted through tightly clenched teeth. From somewhere deep down in her dungarees, she worked up a shriek. Her mouth was full of worm so the shriek had to come out throught her nostrils. Even so, I reckon it was still piercing enough to interfere with television reception. Suddenly I heard somebody else screaming along with her. It was me. She'd practically bitten my index finger in half.

It must have been this double scream that got Sniff away from his usual post by the front gate. He likes to hide behind it until people go by and then he throws himself against the railings at the top so that they drop their shopping or fall off their bikes. Today, I had noticed him happily occupied, lying in a shallow puddle of water Dad had made when he washed the car. Sniff was amusing himself with what looked to me from a distance like a tea-bag. He was knocking it about with his nose and paws, then tossing it up in the air and catching it in his jaws. Anyway, he came charging down the side-passage and when he saw me struggling with Sal, trying to get my bitten finger out of her mouth, he immediately rushed back a few feet, gathered up his tea-bag again and then came bounding up to us on the lawn, woofing hysterically, yiking like locked brakes and trying to squeeze his tea-bag in between us.

It was not my day at all. First my sister ate one of

my best worms. Then she sank her choppers into my fingers so hard she made it bleed. Finally, Sniff bounced at me, caught me off-balance and I slipped and smacked my head on the ground.

I was dizzy for a second, but I could tell Sniff was still pounding about, trying to play, because he made little charging, growling runs at me as I lay on the grass and every now and then he butted me in the ribs with his nose or with a big paw. As I slowly opened my eyes, I focused on the bedroom window of the house next door. There, behind the net curtains, I could clearly see the pale face of Miss Morris, her bulging eyes registering total horror.

*

Dad says he reckons Miss Morris was brought up in India and had a nanny. I think this is quite likely because there are a lot of things she doesn't seem to know about. For one thing, she doesn't know much about dogs or fights. If you've ever been one of a crowd watching a nice little scrap, and everybody is shouting 'Fight! Fight!', you'll know that you can't stand there long without giving the kid next to you a bit of a rough-up too. You know, your arms sort of *automatically* go round his neck and then you have a roll round and a good bit of friendly duffing up. Poor old Miss Morris. She was probably never *allowed* to enjoy a good scrap – so how could she work out for herself that Sniff had got into the fight between Sal and me for the doggy equivalent of a laugh? What she thought she saw from her upstairs window was the brutal attack by a mad and rather untidy Hound of the Baskervilles on two defenceless young kiddi-winks who were so terrified that they were clinging together for support.

Anyway, I was sitting up, seeing how many drops of blood I could squeeze from the toothmarks in my injured finger, when Miss Morris arrived in the garden. She looked even more wild-eyed than usual and was waving a hefty great walking-stick over her head. She had a great collection of sticks in an umbrella stand in her hall. I saw it once through her letterbox when she was out.

'Get back, you brute!' she shouted. 'Leave! Leave!'

Sniff was delighted to carry on with the game. He took a flying leap and grabbed Miss Morris's raised walking-stick and then he was off. He charged round the garden with it, doing a fair bit of damage, first to the sunflowers, then to the runner beans, pausing now and then to give the walking-stick a shake in case there was any life left in it. He got it caught up in the strings supporting the tomato-plants and soon he was dragging a couple of their bamboo canes with him into the flower-bed. He ploughed in among the chrysanthemums, flattening most of them and scattering their petals about like coloured snow.

When he'd done two or three lunatic circuits, he returned to give Miss Morris a chance to grab the stick and a really thorough bumping and sniffling at the same time, just to show how grateful he was to her for being such a surprisingly good sport.

Miss Morris's reaction to this was to throw her arms in a protective knot across her ears and eyes and to bend double. Personally, I would never have tried anything like that with Sniff. He'd had a couple of nasty experiences with hedgehogs in the garden, so he'd learned that in some cases the softly-softly approach was less painful. But just because he wasn't going to be rough, it didn't mean that he wasn't going to do something rude. He dropped the walking-stick and crouched down. It was lucky that my mind had

now cleared completely since the crack to my head, and that I was able to figure out what his next move would be. He was going to try to uncurl her by poking his powerful nose up under that tempting, tweed-skirted bottom. Something told me that Miss Morris would not see the funny side of this and, just in time, I distracted him by shaking the walking-stick under his chin. He immediately grabbed it between his teeth and worried it fiercely for a moment or two – until he suddenly caught sight of his tea-bag and decided that it was more interesting. He pounced on it and shook it like a rat.

All this gave Miss Morris the opportunity to uncurl herself of her own accord, while I did my best to sit on what I could get hold of of the panting, rasping Sniffy-Boy. Sal thought this was dead funny and sat gurgling with laughter while mud and chewed worm dribbled on to her T-shirt. Perhaps because part of what I had been sitting on was head (it was always difficult to tell with Sniff), he was in need of a bit of air when I got off him. That was why he was kicking out so wildly, I suppose. Still, it didn't explain his spluttering and coughing and the litres of white froth coming out of his mouth.

Have you ever seen one of those films where the eyes in a painting move as the hero creeps among the suits of armour towards the secret passage? That was how Miss Morris's eyes moved in her drained and frozen face as they took in the foaming jaws of Sniff and then the smears of blood on my thumb and forefinger.

'He's bitten you!' she whispered. 'He's drawn blood! And look at his mouth . . .!' she mouthed, as though she didn't want Sniff to hear. Then she added, '. . . dear.'

Dear, eh? This was laying it on a bit thick. But then I thought – aha! She's trying to soften me up so that I'll tell her where Mum is. Cunning, eh? Because when you tell people like Miss Morris where your Mum is, they go and tell them about something you've been up to and then you get into trouble for it. I had to get the old brain working quickly. What had I done recently that she wanted to get me for? Looking through her letterbox, maybe? Anyway, I had to do some quick thinking.

'She's – er – not here,' I said I thought that was pretty good on the spur of the moment because she obviously *wasn't*. I didn't want to be more precise and say that she had gone to the library because I felt that Miss Morris might hang around and boss us about. Anyhow, Dad was looking after us – except that he was in the garage – but I certainly wasn't going to mention it to Miss Morris. I happened to know that he was stripping down the carburettor on the car, which is a dead fiddly job, and I know he doesn't like to be disturbed while he's concentrating.

'Dreadful,' she said. 'How dreadful.' She seemed uncertain what to do next but suddenly she took a deep breath. She decided something. 'Don't worry,' she said with great dignity, in spite of the fact that something had come undone in her hair and she was looking a bit freaky. 'Don't worry. *I* shan't abandon you. I shall be no more than a few minutes.'

At that, she left the garden at a speed that startled Sniff so much that he leapt to his feet and scrambled towards her. Luckily, I caught him by the tail and, before he got his great paws properly untangled, managed to hang on to him while, with a whimper and an extra little spurt, Miss Morris sprinted down the side-passage in what I should think was a record-breaking time. I gave my injured finger a soothing suck.

'What dat?' asked Sal, pointing at Sniff who was frantically trying to scrape froth from round his head with his front legs.

'Cuckoo-spit,' I said, confidently. 'He probably ate some when he dived into the hedge just now.'

'What tootoo pit?' Sal enquired. I was going to flash my knowledge at her. We'd done frog-hoppers in Biology. I was trying to work out a way of explaining to her how the nymphs of certain insects, and particularly the frog-hopper, protect themselves by making little frothy nests among the leaves, when it occurred to me that it might not be the right time of the year. The something told me that she wasn't really interested in cuckoo-spit, because she was crawling at full speed towards my worm-box again. And as I dashed off to stop her messing about with my experiment, something else occured to me. The ragged tea-bag that lay on the lawn by the still-frothing Sniff was not in fact a tea-bag at all. It was actually an empty sachet of Turtle Wax car shampoo.

'Aha!' I said out loud. Another case wrapped up by the great Sherlock Moore!

*

When Mum got home from the library, she stood in the garden as if she was visiting some ruin and trying to figure out where everything was when it was all there. I think she was quite pleased when she came through the front door with her books and saw the vase of chrysanthemums on the hall table. But when she came through into the kitchen and saw that there were another six vases full and some others with sunflowers, tomato-plants and runner beans in, you could tell she thought this was a bit of a bummer.

'But why did you *do* this, guys?' she said, looking hopelessly round the garden. I could tell this was serious and that she was beginning to think she had failed as a Mother. (I had heard her getting uptight about this before, when she and Dad were talking about how Sal kept wetting her knickers – but don't ask me what that had to do with failing as a mother.) Anyhow, I decided to explain how Miss Morris had just wandered in and got the dog going.

'How do you mean, Ben,"*got the dog going*"?'

'He too excited,' put in Sal, who had a lot of experience of being Too Excited.

'Miss Morris came in and gave him a stick,' I explained, 'And that sort of wound him up.'

'Miss Morris? Miss Morris came in? Miss Morris never comes in. She hardly speaks to us. Why would she want to come into our garden?'

'She lookin for you,' said Sal.

'Yes,' I said. 'I told her you weren't here and then she said 'How dreadful' or something and not to worry, she'd be back.'

Mum blushed. One second she was looking pale and the next she was all red. She snatched up Sal and cuddled her. 'But I was only gone for twenty minutes. I told you where I was going, and Dad knew where I was. I was only down the road at the library, wasn't I? I offered to take you but you said you preferred to stay and look after Sniff. Where is he, by the way? And where's Dad?'

'In the garage,' I said.

'With Radio 3 blaring away, I expect,' said Mum, angrily.

'Miff hidin,' Sal said.

'Why is Sniff hiding, Ben?'

'Ben naughty!' Sal said. 'He squirt Miff wid da hose-pie. Miff all wet.'

At this moment, the Whee-whee-whee! and the Dah-da, Dah-da! that had been going on in the background became very loud and close. There was a squeal of brakes, doors slammed, and Sniff, who, since I had hosed him down, had gone to hide in the house somewhere, suddenly came zooming out of the back door and charged down the side-passage to see what was going on out in the road. Seconds later, he was charging back. He threw himself down on the lawn behind Mum where she was standing, still clutching Sal, and hid his head up her dress.

We all stood dead still. I was listening so hard I could hear whistling in my ears – and then we heard the slow crunching of gravel under boots.

The first thing that came into sight was a large, trembling net. When he saw it, Sniff began to shake violently and tried to hide himself further under Mum's skirt.

'Now don't panic, madam,' came the nervous voice of the policeman from behind the folds of the net.

'Where's the dog? Can you see it yet?' hissed a deeper voice from behind him.

'Can't see it yet, Sarge,' said the policeman. 'Only the woman and the kids.'

'We'll soon have you safe, madam,' confided the voice of the hidden Sergeant. 'We've got an ambulance for the boy and PC Fuller will – er – see to the dog. Everything's just fine. Just take your time and bring the kiddies round to the front of the house . . .'

'You can't take them away from me,' wailed Mum. 'I didn't *leave* them. I was only gone for twenty minutes. And anyway, their dad was here all the time. I just went to the library. We wouldn't leave them alone, honestly. You see, Ben was here to keep an eye on my little girl, and he's a very sensible boy, so what was the harm in . . .I mean, they didn't want to come . . . It was only this once . . . We're really careful about things like that. I mean, we never *neglect* them or anything . . . Can't you just leave them here with me . . . and their dad? I don't know what Miss Morris has told you but . . . I only went to the library . . .'

'Never mind about libraries, madam. Be reasonable. They're not safe here, are they?' cooed the Sergeant. 'And when you come to think about it, *you're* not safe either, are you? Not with the dog in that state. Much better if you just come very quietly with us. What d'you say?'

'What do you mean? In what *state*? What's wrong with the dog?' said Mum.

'Oh my Gawd!' yelled PC Fuller, interrupting.

'What's up?' yelled the Sergeant.

'It's behind her!'

'Right, Fuller, move in! Grab the brute!' The Sergeant gave his hesitant colleague a shove and they both spilled on to the patio and into the garden.

When PC Fuller lifted his net, Sniff realized that he only wanted to play. He dashed out from his hiding place (still looking rather damp, from the hosing down I'd given him to get the froth off, so poor Mum must have been rather uncomfortable) and, just as he had done when Miss Morris lifted her walking-stick, he jumped up, grabbed the net and tore off round the garden.

Dad arrived just in time to see Sniff pounding

about the garden like some mobile windmill, demolishing most of what he hadn't already knocked down with Miss Morris's walking-stick.

*

There was, as they say, a certain amount of explaining to do. Quite a number of policemen, firemen and ambulance men had to be given tea. Most of them refused rosehip and camomile and settled for Earl Grey. They sat around, sniffing at the steaming brew and raising their eyebrows appreciatively before getting out their notebooks and taking down 'the facts'. Miss Morris couldn't be persuaded to have anything and wouldn't stay long. She kept apologizing for dialling 999 under false pretences. It was the mad behaviour that had worried her and the froth round his mouth. The policemen, the ambulance men and the firemen blew on their Earl Grey and said that it was important that the public called them if they were suspicious because rabies was very nasty, very nasty and you never knew.

After she'd gone, they all sat round, laughing a lot, having their mugs refilled and eating all the biscuits, even the Wholemeal Carob Crunch which were expensive because they came from the health food shop. Some of the men made a note of the name and took a couple more, and I think Mum was quite pleased in a way.

They all made a fuss of Sniff which made Sal a bit jealous so she showed off and wet her knickers. I thought of asking loudly for an Elastoplast for my finger but then I thought it was definitely nobler to suffer in silence.

'He do look a bit nuts, dun he?' mused the Sergeant, giving Sniff a good scratch and winking at PC Fuller who blushed, probably thinking about his net. Sniff woofed in agreement and was rewarded by a shower of chocolate fingers from the fire brigade who wanted to give him a scratch too.

Dad didn't say much. I think he was a bit cheesed off about the flowers and the vegetables. I don't suppose he would have minded at all if Sniff had destroyed the nettles up the far end that Mum insisted on keeping to encourage butterflies. Anyway, I had an idea and asked the Chief Fireman if I could have a quick look over his fire engine. Dad cheered up when he heard this. A keen look came to his eyes. While the Chief was still nodding, I asked if Dad could have a look too.

The Chief looked a bit uncertain. 'That wouldn't put you out, would it, sir?'

'Absolutely not!' said Dad. 'I'd love to have a look round, if that's all right with you. We haven't had a close look at that particular model, have we Ben?'

'Right, then!' said the Chief, rubbing his hands together. You could tell he didn't often get real enthusiasts like us. 'We've got one or two special features I think will interest you. All set?'

'Ready when you are!' said Dad. So that was all right.

*

When we came back into the kitchen, Mum had done most of the clearing up and Sal was sitting in her chair, finishing off the last of the Carob Crunch biscuits.

'You all right now, love?' said Dad. She had been a bit emotional after the Emergency Services had all kissed her goodbye.

'I'm fine, love, thanks,' she said, but her chin was wobbling a bit. 'And I think it was jolly brave of Miss Morris to come into the garden at all, actually. After all, she thought Ben and Sal were being attacked by a mad dog.'

'You're right, love,' Dad agreed. 'I think maybe we ought to give her a little something to show our appreciation.'

'What about a bunch of chrysanthemums?' I suggested, which I thought was brill but Dad didn't seem too keen.

'Ben, old son,' he said, giving me one of his over-the-top-of-the-glasses looks, 'don't push your luck.'

*

When I got into bed that night, I discovered where Sniff had gone to hide after I hosed him down – but I thought I'd rather keep quiet about it and put up with a bit of dampness – what with one thing and another.

Sniff Makes the News

Sal and her little friend, Tom, were painting. They were standing on the back of one of the sofas in the sitting-room, painting the windows with tomato sauce. Sniff was sitting on the sofa, helping. He licked up most of the sauce that dropped on to the sofa and, when they would let him, he licked the hands of the painters – who happened to be painting with their fingers. Tom let him lick his hands most because he liked being tickled with a hot rubbery tongue almost as much as he liked painting windows with tomato sauce. Sal preferred to concentrate on painting. After all, she could get her hands licked any time she had anything worth licking on them.

I was a bit worried about the wild noise Tom made every time he got licked, in case he brought Bunty (his mum) and my mum in from the kitchen. Mum and Bunty were writing a protest song and didn't want to be interrupted, and I didn't want to be interrupted just at the point where I was approaching my best-ever score at *Swampbeast*. I had no more than a dozen Slimeswine to zap when I sensed that my record-breaking attempt was about to end in failure. I sensed it because all of a sudden Sniff, who until then had been content to slurp tomato sauce more or less quietly, suddenly started howling like a wolf. For a second, I thought that one of the weenie ones had dropped the sauce bottle on his head. I soon realized that this was not the case, because normally when people drop things on his head he runs round the room and knocks everything over. He did not run round the room. He sat where he was on the sofa with his head thrown back and he kept on howling, higher and spookier; more like an owl than a wolf, more like a siren or a tug-boat whistle than coyote, but with a touch of all of those. It got your attention, if you know what I mean.

It got Mum's attention and Bunty's. One second they were just peacefully sitting in the kitchen, jingle-jangling on their guitars and singing – Mum singing the tune and Bunty doing the high harmony bit. Next thing they knew, it sounded as though their little tinies were being pushed slowly through a food processor.

I should explain why Mum and Bunty were writing songs. They quite often do this. Some of them are

OK, and I agree about saving whales and protecting the ozone layer and all that. The trouble is, I can't stand the wobbly way Bunty sings. And, she has those SMILE stickers all over her guitar.

Anyway, they'd got together this song that went:

> We don't want no vivisection
> Nor does Rat or Bunny
> If a rat gave you an injection
> You wouldn't think it was funny.

Then there was a harmonica solo. That was where they'd got to. They didn't get any further because at that point, as soon as Bunty blew and sucked the first couple of notes on her mouth-organ, Sniff came out with his horrendous howl.

I was really cheesed off, of course. It was the end of my peace and quiet and wrecked my attempt at zapping a record number of Slimeswine. And there they were, Mum and Bunty standing in the room panting, expecting to see some terrible accident.

'Ben, why didn't you *stop* them?' Mum said, forgetting her anxieties about the weenies in a flash and seeing nothing but the sauce-smeared windows and the red globs on the sofa that Sniff had missed.

I tried to explain about how important it is for small kids to be creative and not frustrated all the time (I'd heard her say this to Dad once when he took his claw-hammer away from Sal) but she wasn't listening. She was scrubbing at the sofa with wet kitchen towel while Bunty was giving Sal and Tom a heavy wash in the kitchen sink. Sniff, who had stopped howling as soon as the anxious mums appeared, had done the dirty and sloped off, leaving me to face the music.

'That's really irresponsible, Ben. Really selfish,' Mum was saying above the distinctly different howls of the weenies getting washed. 'You were supposed to be looking after them. You just wait till you want to do something really important and I shall come and interrupt *you*.'

'I *was* doing something important,' I said, but she obviously thought song writing came higher up the list of priorities than perfecting your skills as a Swampbeast Buster.

*

At about seven o'clock that evening, I was holding the soldering iron for Dad, who was repairing the printed circuit of an old radio. It was always good to be in the garage when there were bad vibes in the house. You could get your mind on something interesting and forget your problems. There were one or two small bits of supper on Dad's chin but he wasn't bothered; he was concentrating. He was peering through a magnifying glass at the flat silver trail of the circuit, looking for gaps. I fizzed a bit of solder on the bench while Dad wiggled a transistor with a pair of snub-nosed pliers to see if it had come loose.

'The trouble is,' he explained, 'your mum's a bit struck for something to do at the Animal Rights demo at the weekend.' I remembered now. They were going to demonstrate outside a fur shop in the high street. 'She and Bunty were going to do the posters but that other woman – the one with the ginger hair – seems to have got in there before them. What *is* her name. . . ?'

'Hermione,' I said.

'Thanks,' Dad said, taking the soldering iron. 'Yes, that's her. She's done these amazing banner-things and your mum's a bit narked. She and Bunty have spent ages trying to come up with something really impressive, something that'll really get people's attention. Know what I mean? They think the telly might be there.'

'They're not planning to sing on the telly, are they?' I said. I was shocked. 'What happens if my friends see Mum with *her*?'

'Who, Bunty? Now come on, Ben. What's wrong with her? She's a very nice lady and she's very sincere.'

'I know that,' I said. 'But, Dad, she wears ginormous flares . . . and she's got stickers on her guitar, and that "Prefect" badge on her duffle coat.

What are people at school going to say if they see my mum with her?'

'Don't be so daft,' said Dad. 'It's ridiculous to judge people by what they look like. Anyway, be honest,' he went on, 'how many of your friends watch the news?'

'Thurston,' I said, 'for one.'

'Ah, yes . . .' Dad had forgotten about Thurston. 'But anyway, you ought to be proud of your mum. She's doing something really worthwhile. I think you should go along with her and – well, help her out.'

'What!'

'Now you know I would if I could, but I told you, I can't miss that conference in Birmingham. There are going to be crowds of other engineers there and I can't afford to miss out on recent trends, can I?' I had to agree, but I couldn't help thinking that if Dad kept up with what's cool and what's uncool as well as he did with laser technology and super-conductors, he wouldn't leave me to suffer like this. 'You've got nothing vital on,' he went on. 'Why don't you go and demonstrate, and help her and Bunty strike a blow for creatures that can't protect themselves?' He blew on the connection he had soldered with the strength of someone who had just said something pretty final.

'I would, Dad, but they'll . . . well, there won't be any men there. And what happens if the shop-bloke comes out and starts making a fuss? It'll all be dead embarrassing.'

'You worry too much about being embarrassed,' Dad said, fitting the back on the mended radio. 'And if the owner's embarrassed, that's excellent. That'll make him think again about trading in the skins of the innocent.'

*

If anything, when the day of the demo came, it was worse than I'd imagined it could be. For one thing, it was drizzling. This meant that when Bunty turned up with Tom to collect Mum, she was wearing this green Paddington Bear coat, a purple beanie hat, blue wellies and these waterproof orange trousers with *huge* flares. Talk about ding-dong. I didn't know *where* to look. And I couldn't pretend I wasn't with her because there weren't enough of us to get lost among. I tried to think of some way to hide my face if the television cameras turned up. A balaclava? That would be ideal but Sniff had eaten mine. An umbrella! That was it. But guess who hadn't got a hand free for an umbrella because his responsibility was to hold on to the pushchairs and the dog, *and* keep an eye on the guitars because certain other people had important placards to carry . . .

There were about ten of us altogether outside A la Mode Furs, including the Telly. The Telly consisted of two incredibly bored-looking blokes, one with a backpack and a hefty video camera and the other with a shoulder-bag full of sound equipment and ear-phones slung round his neck. They paid a lot of attention to lighting up their roll-your-own fags but the drizzle kept putting them out. They whispered miserably to each other, hopped from foot to foot to keep warm and looked at their watches all the time.

Mum, Bunty, Hermione and two other women, lugged Hermione's rather smartly-printed protests round and round in a circle outside the shop of shame. One of the placards had written on it ONLY DUMB ANIMALS WEAR FUR, which I had to admit was pretty good. Nothing happened. Nobody came out of the shop. The owner had obviously decided that the best thing he could do was keep his head down. Maybe he hadn't even come in to work. When we first arrived, a young assistant came and squinted out at us through the glass of the door. That was it. He didn't do anything – smile or scowl or wave or tell us to buzz off. He just stood behind the glass door for a couple of seconds, looked bored and then sauntered back behind his counter – or wherever he'd come from. There were one or two shoppers in the high street but when they saw us they all scurried away looking rather sheepish. Hermione led the women in a bit of chanting but the men from the telly were not impressed. They didn't bother to get the camera working.

'If something doesn't happen soon, they'll go away,' said Hermione out of the corner of her mouth to the damp woman beside her. 'And all this effort will be wasted.' She and the damp woman both knew she was talking about *her* banners and placards, rather than the efforts of the rest of us who had taken the trouble to turn out on a horrible wet Saturday morning to protest. Still, it did seem a waste of time if nobody was even going to notice us.

Sal and Tom were getting a bit restless in their pushchairs in the doorway of the shop next door to A la Mode Furs, and Sniff was whining and shivering and yawning. A few drops of rain drummed miserably on to the guitar cases until I footed them a bit further into the shop doorway.

'It's up to us now,' said Bunty firmly, with a determined sort of Girl Guide look at Mum. 'I think a song is called for, don't you?' She took Mum's placard that read MINK JUST NATURALLY STINK! PEOPLE SHOULD KNOW BETTER! and leant it against the shop window beside Sal. Then she leant her own placard beside Tom. Within a minute, she and Mum were ping-pinging their guitars into tune and Tom and Sal were amusing themselves by knocking the placards over so that I had to pick them up again.

I saw Bunty slipping a wire harness over her head. It was a thing for holding a mouth-organ when you have to use both hands to play your guitar. As I watched her hitching her guitar-strap over her shoulder and pursing her lips to test the distance of the mouth-organ, I suddenly realized something. I remembered what had put an end to my Slimeswine zapping record. Because I'd been concentrating like mad on my record-breaking attempt at the time, I had hardly been aware of precisely what it was that caused Sniff to attempt his imitation of the Hound of the Baskervilles. But now, instantly, I knew – it was *Bunty's mouth-organ*!

Mum and Bunty strummed their guitars and sang the first verse of 'Fur Traders' Blues' and then Bunty started to suck and blow on the mouth-organ. They'd got to the instrumental chorus and as the first of the throbbing, vibrating notes bounced off the shop windows, Sniff reacted as if someone had plugged his tail into an electric socket.

'*Whoo ooo dooo Wahooo dooo Weoow*,' he wailed.

The effect on the camera team was equally electrifying. Up came the camera on to the cameraman's shoulder in about two seconds. In the same instant, the sound man flipped away his soggy roll-up, unslung his earphones from his neck and clapped them over his ears. They crawled towards our doorway, pointing lens and mike at the upthrust nose of Sniff.

Bunty and Mum stopped.

'Keep going, lady! Keep going with the harmonica!' he urged.

She was a little reluctant, now that the camera was not on her, but obliged with a suck-blow-suck that was hardly less enthusiastic than before. Off went Sniff into another ear-splitting series of howls. Tom and Sal very quickly got into the spirit of the thing.

'*Wo-woooooo! Wo-woooooo-woooooo-woooooo*!' they sang.

'That's terrific!' wheezed the sound man. 'Is this your dog?'

'He myse,' said Sal. 'He singin.'

'What's he singing about, sweetheart?' said the cameraman.

'Non't know,' said Sal. She'd gone all shy.

'What about this little chap?' the cameraman said to Tom.

'Nahh,' said Tom, who hardly ever says anything else.

'Ben know what he singin,' said Sal.

'Are you Ben?' asked the cameraman, pointing the lens in my direction. I nodded.

'What's he singing about, Ben?' said the cameraman eagerly, twisting the lens to get me in close-up.

'Well, roughly translated,' I yelled above the howling which Tom and Sal had decided to sing along with again, 'what he's saying is – he doesn't want anyone nicking *his* fur coat and hanging it up in a shop window.'

Quite a little crowd had gathered by now. The cameraman took them in in a swift sweeping motion, came back to capture the singing doggy and the chorus of wailing weenies, and the protesting ladies who had shouldered their banners again, and Mum and Bunty who were strumming away like anything.

'That's it!' called the cameraman, and to the sound man, 'Cut!' He heaved his camera off his shoulder and let it hang like a suitcase. 'Thanks very much, everybody,' he called as he and his mate both ran to a small van that was parked nearby and hissed away through the drizzle.

*

Thurston rang to congratulate me after the television news item beginning, 'Children and a wonderful singing dog won hearts and minds today in a High Street protest.'

'Did you make that stuff up, or did they train you to say it?' he enquired. Typical of Thurston's suspicious mind, that. 'And how did you get that idiot dog of yours to perform? Were you standing on his tail or something?'

I explained about the mouth-organ but he didn't believe me.

'Hang on a sec,' he said, and I could hear him rummaging about in a drawer. He was, of course, speaking from his *personal* extension in his 'study'. Bedrooms are not enough for Thurston. A couple of moments later and he was back, oozing smugness into the phone. 'Right,' he said. 'Got one. I knew I had one somewhere. Let's give it a go, shall we? Where's the mutt?'

'Asleep on the rug about three metres away.'

'OK. You hold the phone towards him and I'll give this thing a quick blow. It's a harmonica, actually, by the way, not a mouth-organ.'

'Same thing,' I said and ignored his squeaky little know-all reply. 'Just blow the thing, will you?' I said and held the receiver out at arm's length. The result was that Sniff went off like a police siren.

Mum and Dad were not amused by the demonstration, of course, and cut it short with some language which you don't expect from responsible parents.

'Hmm,' came Thurston's voice, grudgingly. 'But don't imagine I didn't see that woman with your mother. The one with the badges and the ding-dongs. What a wally!'

'You ought to know better than to judge people by appearances,' I said, knowing that Thurston would think that was a feeble answer. 'Anyway, you're just jealous.'

'Ding-dong,' said Thurston as I put the phone down on him.

'Mum!' I called. 'Have you seen that book Thurston lent me?'

'It's somewhere in the sitting-room,' she called back, 'unless you moved it.'

'Thanks,' I said and started rummaging. I wanted to find it so that I could give it to Sniff to chew.

Shopping with Sniff

We have a V W Passat estate. I've told Dad about it but we've still got it. Thurston's family have got a B M W. I only know one other family that's got a more embarrassing car than we have and they're teachers, so there you are. Mum says we've got to have an estate because they're useful.

It was Saturday morning. I was thinking about how *useful* it would be to own a B M W that did nought to sixty in 6.3 seconds. Then I wouldn't have had to stand whistling, with my hands in my pockets, outside Miss Morris's next door, trying to pretend to people passing by that I didn't have anything to do with our car.

Mum finished strapping Sal in, banged the door on her noise, walked round to the other side of the car and held the other back door open – for me. Sal's screams poured out all over the street again. Miss Morris's curtains were twitching. Not far behind them, Miss Morris must have been twitching, too.

'Get in,' Mum said, in quite a tense sort of way, showing a lot of teeth. I once saw a film about Lord Nelson, and when the ship's surgeon sawed his wounded arm off, Lord Nelson had a smile a bit like Mum's.

She was looking kind of flushed, standing beside the car. Dad was behind the wheel, trying to get the seat to move back and also looking rather hot and bothered. Sal was in the back, kicking wildly in the safety chair where Mum had just strapped her. She was screaming fit to burst and looking *well* stewed. Sniff was rushing round and round in the boot-space like a record of Sal's scream going round on a turntable. His tongue was right out because *he* was *super*-heated.

Meanwhile, I thought I was quite cool. I stood for a bit longer by Miss Morris's gate, even after Mum said 'Get in the car!' with her face all squeezed up. Then I started to wander in their general direction. Finally, Mum came over and sort of guided me in by the back of my neck. I thought it was unnecessary but I decided to rise above it and say nothing.

One of the things I don't like about our car is that it doesn't smell like normal cars do. What it does smell like is a fridge that's got a couple of sprouts going sludgy under the salad tray. I mean, I don't mind that sort of smell in a fridge, but the inside of a car should smell of plastic and stuff. Another thing is, I prefer non-stick seats. Jam's OK but I'm not all that keen on sitting on it. And another thing is, I like to be able to see things through the windows. Sal and Sniff manage to get so much smear and smudge and spit all over the glass that looking out is a bit like trying to see into somebody's bathroom.

At least I had a bit more room than usual. That was only because Dad couldn't get the seat back from Mum's driving position. He had his knees up on either side of the steering-wheel and his elbows out sideways. The car lurched forward, stopped and jumped again. Sal stopped screaming.

'Sorry, guys. Can't get the old foot up,' Dad said.

'Do it adain!' Sal said and squawked with pleasure as the engine roared and we bunnyhopped another few metres.

Mum and Dad decided to change places and Sal amused herself by trying to remove handfuls of my hair.

'Be nice to her, Ben. She's only a little girl,' said Dad as soon as I tried to stop her. That's another thing I don't like about our car – it's not fair.

We were going to the supermarket, so, as far as I was concerned, things could only get worse. The plan had been to try to get there early to beat the rush, but Sal had wet herself at the last minute and held things up so now, when we arrived at the car park, it was more or less full. We had to wait hours for someone to come out and move a car, and it was getting hotter and hotter and cars were arriving all the time and lining up behind us and hooting. Mum was dead cheesed off about it but eventually she managed to find a spot right over in the corner away from the main entrance to the supermarket.

'You sure that's OK, darling?' she said to Dad who had got out to guide her in.

'Tons of room, love. Any fool can get round you there,' he said confidently.

Mum took the point and, with a bit of grunting and struggling and revving, squeezed the car into the space Dad had recommended. 'Leave your window open for Sniff,' Mum said to me, switching off the engine. 'I'll put some water in his dish.'

Sniff seemed to have exhausted himself by turning round and round. Or maybe it was the heat or something. Anyway, he stood quietly while Mum poured some water out of a plastic bottle into his dish and he didn't put up the usual fight to get out of the car. He put his tongue in the water to cool, gave it a couple of slap-slaps and lay down.

'Good boy,' said Mum, banging down the tailgate. 'You have a little snooze. We won't be long.'

Sniff gave her a one-eyed look and banged the side-panels twice with his tail before flopping over sideways and doing his favourite imitation of a rug.

'Naughty boy!' said Sal from under Dad's arm, as if she knew something that Mum and Dad didn't. But Sniff didn't wiggle a whisker.

★

I hate shopping. I hate shopping in supermarkets even more, and most of all I hate shopping with the whole family in a supermarket. It's dead embarrassing. I was worried in case any of my friends from school saw me out shopping. Of course, most of them were at home watching TV but one or two of them might have gone by on a bike. I needn't have worried. There was hardly anyone there who wasn't really old, apart from other weenies like Sal, that is.

It was horrible. Miles of shelves. Nothing to do. Too many people wandering about to let you get a good run and find out how slippery the floor was. Every time I saw something good, like a Black Forest gateau or a big bag of Mars Bars, I got a lecture on E-numbers. I wasn't allowed to get my own trolley and scoot it about, and Mum and Dad kept sending me off to look for things they'd forgotten.

Typical Supermarket Conversation:

'Blast! Soap. Ben. Soap.'

'Where is it?'

'Oh, come on. Use your loaf.'

(Ten minutes later.) 'This do?'

'Don't be ridiculous, that's pink.'

'So?'

'We never have pink soap. Haven't you ever noticed what colour the bathroom is? Go and get plain white or green.'

(Ten minutes later.) 'This do?'

'Is that all they've got? No, forget it. Put that back. I'll get some at The Body Shop later.'

This can be very wearing. Thurston told me that you can sue your parents for child-abuse over things like that, but I decided against mentioning this just then because Sal had opened a packet of spaghetti and Dad was agreeing with the Deputy Manager that he'd have to pay for it even though most of it was on the floor.

'Of course I shall pay for it,' Dad said. 'As soon as we get to the checkout.'

I'm not exactly sure what couth is but I don't think the Deputy Manager was, even though he was wearing a badge that said DEPUTY MANAGER. I didn't like him much. He had a dew-drop hanging from his nose and ginger eyebrows that met in the middle. He'd just made a trolley-boy blush in front of the customers for being thirty seconds late back from his tea-break. Now he turned round to have a go at some poor girl-assistant for not sticking labels on tins of tomatoes quickly enough. The Deputy Manager was the type who is constantly on the lookout for Trouble with a capital T.

Down by the fruit and veg, I passed two little kids. One of them was admiring the other, who was pointing his fingers like a gun and going '*Pchhh! Pchhh!*' at the sprouts, cabbage and broccoli.

He stopped when he saw me watching him and looked a bit worried; so did his friend. 'He only kills the ones he don't like,' explained the little kid who wasn't shooting. He obviously thought I might tell on his friend if he started murdering potatoes. A small onion had been dropped in the aisle. I booted it under the vegetable rack and hung about just long enough to see both kids scuttling after their mums to tell on me. Then I walked off, trying to look *well* hard, but I half wondered if the Deputy Manager would get me for it. He was over by the bread counter, shouting at an old lady with blue hair for blocking the gangway. 'You wanna get a move on, lady!' he was shouting. 'There're other people trying to shop as well as you, you know.' Even so, I was still a bit worried in case he had me on video.

I found Mum counting bottles of Perrier water on to the trolley. I tried to sneak a bottle of Coca Cola on board with them. She noticed, gave me a pitying look as if I had part of my brain missing and put it back on the shelf.

'Oh, Mum, why not? It's so hot!' I said, trying to sound reasonable, though I must admit it came out more like a whine. Actually, I was hoping that she would be too whacked out to put up a struggle, but I underestimated her stamina and Dad's. They gave me their complete attention and a very loud five minute lecture on Cola Attack. My mouth would fill with plaque and my teeth would fill with craters. Phosphoric acid would eat away at the enamel. I would be kept awake all night by caffeine and would probably go hyper like Thurston. I would develop a terrible craving for the stuff and lose all self control about my diet in general. I would start wanting to spend all my time in McDonald's like Cindy and Tristram Stewart.

Several people nearby were genuinely shocked by this flood of info and I noticed that two of them, looking dead guilty, drifted away from the soft drinks shelves without choosing anything. One woman refused to be put off, however.

‘ ’Scuse me,’ she said loudly and swung four two-litre bottles on to her trolley. I suppose that’s what you call knowing your own mind.

Dad bent down and whispered to me, ‘See what a fat bottom she’s got? Coca Cola addict,’ and gave me a nod and a nudge.

By now, I was really fed up. Mum had decided to *study* the vegetables one by one as if they were things from outer space. Dad had gone in search of kitchen foil. Sal managed to get a handful of watercress into her mouth and green gunge was running down the front of her frock as she spluttered and spat and tried to rake the stuff off her tongue with her finger-nails. Mum was complaining to another woman that you can’t get fresh coriander in supermarkets.

It was when at last lining up – at checkout 5 – that I suddenly realized that Sniff had arrived.

I was not the only one to realize this. Sniff can get through a crowd like a snowplough through a snow drift. From where we were by the checkout, we couldn’t see the people in Aisle 1 – which is where you start from the car-park entrance. What I *could* see were their hands going up in the air, some of them clutching cereal packets and other items of grocery, as they flattened themselves against the shelves. I could also see the shocked faces of the people at the end of the row, turning towards the disaster that they sensed was moving rapidly towards them.

It was only a couple of microseconds after I noticed the human wave that I noticed the sound. Distantly at first, like far-off tea-trays dropped in remote kitchens, I could hear the sound of collapsing pyramids of tins. Then came the thud of felled display-cases, followed by the hiss of crashing trolleys. Tottering towers of heaped-up soap powder packets avalanched down with a drumming like hooves. Above the shimmering strings of the music from the loudspeakers came the wails of the shocked and the knocked-down customers.

When Sniff came into sight, just past the cheese counter, he started jumping over the trolleys that were lined up at the checkout counters. He was like a great hairy horse clearing the last four fences at The Grand National. As he approached the last trolley, he was tiring just slightly. Up he went at the gallop, his tongue streaming out like a rasher of bacon. It was a brave effort but his big forefeet clipped the trolley on the side and, with a great spurt of shopping, sent it smashing sideways. As the last of the dried peas rattled and clicked and bounced on the tiles, and the last of the tins rumbled under a counter, the loudspeaker music suddenly cut out with a crackle. For a second, there was only one sound that could be heard in the whole expanse of that store and that was the panting of Sniff. As he stood on his hind legs and licked the green gunge of Sal's face and frock, Sal's welcoming cry was unmistakable,

'Good boy, Miff!'

After that a tinny voice came over the loudspeaker: 'Would the owner of the V W Passat estate, registration number ENG 126, please move it, as it is causing an obstruction in the car park. Thank you.' Dead embarrassing.

What had happened was quite simple. The people parked next to us in the car park had decided that there was no room for them to get by. They were stuck to know what to do when the wife had noticed that our back window on the driver's side was open.

The husband had got her to put her hand through and open the door from the inside. His idea was to get the front door open and release the handbrake so that they could shove the car out of the way. Neither of them had noticed Sniff lying behind the seats, until the back door was open. It was too late then, of course, because he had hopped over the back seat and out of the open door and was off on our trail into the supermarket before you could say 'Minced Doggy Brekko'.

Well, he found us pretty swiftly, you've got to give him that.

The Deputy Manager was delighted. At last, here was some Trouble and he was the man to deal with it. He shouldered aside two gaping shop assistants and advanced, his fat feet crunching broken glass to powder. He stepped over the spilled groceries, avoided the pools of mayonnaise and marmalade, and approached Mum and Dad with his head on one side and his hands on his hips.

He must have been practising in his head what he was going to say. It was going to be something ultra-tough and cool and he opened his mouth to say it. At that same moment, he slipped on a stuffed olive and down he went – KERRRUNCH! on to a carton of eggs. People nearby jumped to avoid being splashed on the ankles by flying gunge.

Somebody laughed. It was the cashier on checkout 5.

When she saw the killer-look under the ginger eyebrows, she clapped her hand across her mouth. Dad bent to help him up but he rudely pushed him away, slapping down the offered hand. As he got to his knees, Sniff moved in close and in a very friendly way, licked the dew-drip right off the man's nose. The Deputy Manager's fist was raised in the air. 'You'll pay for this!' he yelled.

Sniff ran for cover behind Sal who cradled his big, shaggy head in her arms. Someone shouted for the Deputy Manager to leave off.

'Leave him alone, mate!' said the voice. 'He's only a dumb animal!'

The Deputy Manager had got to his feet. 'You keep out of it!' he blazed. 'It's him I'm talking to –

him!' His waggling finger was pointing rudely at Dad. 'I said *you're* going to pay for this!'

'Of course,' said Dad in a very steady voice. He turned to the lady at the cash desk at checkout 5. Her hand was still over her mouth. 'You won't forget to charge me for this, will you?' He held up the packet of spaghetti that Sal had broken open.'I'm afraid my daughter has opened it.'

The Deputy Manager lifted the tail of his jacket and screamed with rage when he saw egg yolk dripping off the seat off his pants and running down his legs. The lady at the cash desk at checkout 5 began to applaud. She couldn't speak. She could only blink away the tears of laughter and clap her hands together. One by one, the other cashiers joined in, and then the two shop assistants who had been shouldered out of the way started to clap and so did the ticked-off trolley-boy and then everyone in the store, hundreds of people, they all started to clap and cheer.

In the middle of all this, the Manager appeared. He was a small, very neat man. His hair was neat, his shoes were very shiny and *his* badge that said MANAGER meant what it said. His neat moustache was bristling.

'Bit of a mess here, Mr Spalding,' he said to the Deputy Manager.

Mr Spalding's ginger eyebrows wriggled with rage.

He spluttered, he puffed, he pointed – but for a second he couldn't actually speak.

Somebody did, though. It was the old lady with the blue hair, the one the Deputy Manager had been rude to for blocking the gangway. 'Harold,' she said.

'Hello, Mother. Nice to see you up and about,' said the Manager.

The Deputy Manager's face went a horrible colour, his mouth fell open and he started at the old lady in terror.

'Harold, I'd like a word with you about *that man*,' she said.

The Deputy Manager began to steam. 'I'll just get this lot cleared up, shall I, sir?' he said. Frantically he started gathering up packets and tins and scattered vegetables. As he bent over, he displayed the vast soggy patch of squidged egg.

'Yes, and then you'd better get yourself cleaned up, I think, Mr Spalding,' said the Manager. 'And after that, I should like to see you in my office. Carry on, everyone.'

Straight away, the tills started bleeping again, and everyone was chatting and helping to put things back on to shelves and picking things up and laughing like old friends and moving through the checkouts. As I said, I hate shopping normally, but I'm glad I didn't miss that outing . . . it was great.

As for Sniff, though, standing there with his fat feet up on our trolley, getting pats on the head and the odd Doggy Choc from complete strangers, I guess he couldn't work out what all the fuss was about.

Sniff and the Pain in the Neck

Sniff turned round and round eight times very fast and fell over. He levered his nose under his crossed front paws and blew hard for a bit. Then he found something that itched in one of the paws and lifted his lip and nibbled at it with his front teeth. This was accompanied by a lot of growling and blowing. If you've ever seen someone eating corn on the cob very fast, you can imagine what he looked like.

After a little bit of paw-gnashing, he was ready to chase his bottom round the other way. I think there's a touch of sheepdog in Sniff somewhere. He likes rounding himself up. When he's out in the car, he always goes in the luggage compartment behind the seats. He never sits down, he just goes round and round or falls over and stays collapsed. He looks out of the side window towards the oncoming traffic. When a car comes, he tries to bite it through the side window and when it's gone past, he tries to bite it through the back window. Each car that comes by is a complete surprise to him and causes him to bang his nose on the side window as he tries to get it. Then he bangs his nose again on the back window as he tries to get his teeth into its exhaust pipe.

If you're not used to having a dog banging its nose (and sometimes clicking its teeth) on the glass, it can be a bit worrying. If there's a lot of traffic, you hear *gathump-gathump-gathump* all the time and you think you've got a flat tyre. Or if there's only the odd car going by, and you're in a bit of a trance, it can be really scary.

It was pretty bad on that Friday evening when Dad picked up me and Thurston from the Leisure Centre. I'd been swimming and Thurston had been to his karate class. His mum and dad thought it would release some of his pent-up energy, but I reckon it made him more hyper than ever. Anyway, that evening, it was drizzling and overcast and we were both sort of out of it. We were sitting there with our mouths open, watching the windscreen wipers going *fizz-fizz*, *fizz-fizz*, *fizz-fizz*. In the background, all we could hear was *ffsssssssshhhh* . . . the sound of the wheels on the wet road. All of a sudden KABAP-KABAP!

'Wah! Wozzat? We've hit something! We've killed a hedgehog!' shouts Thurston.

'Hey, Thurston! Watch it! You're digging your elbow in my ribs. Keep still, for goodness sake!'

'But we've just run over a hedgehog,' he yelled. 'Didn't you hear it get squashed?' He was up, kneeling on the seat and pointing out of the back window at the road. 'There it is! I'm sure I can see it! Yuck!'

'Would you sit down, Thurston,' said my dad. 'You're blocking my view. It's bad enough trying to see past Sniff without having you in the way.'

'Calm down,' I said. 'With my nature-loving dad at the wheel, every little insectivorous quadruped is safe.'

'Well what was that noise then?'

'Nothing, Playdough brain. It was only ickle Sniff Wiffy going wound and wound and biting the nasty trafficky wafficky, wasn't it, my old Snifter?' I put my arm out and gave him a scratch behind the ear and a good hard pat. Sniff wanted some more and put his feet up on the back seat and gave me a panting, slobbery lick. While Dad yelled at him to get down, Thurston threw himself over towards the window on his side. He's always been nervous of dogs.

Poor old Thurston. The neighbourhood hedgehogs may have escaped without damage that evening, but not him. Once Sniff had leapt up on the back seat, he couldn't take his eyes off him. Every time a

car went by and Sniff went into his dancing-doggy routine in the luggage-space, Thurston craned his neck round to watch, to make sure that he wasn't going to get leapt on. By the time we got him home, his neck had seized up and he was stuck with his head turned sideways, and his chin pointing over his left shoulder. Well, he *said* he couldn't move it, but it's hard to tell when Thurston's putting it on.

The following day, I gave Thurston a call. It was ten thirty.

'Hello, Mrs Wilder. Thirsty up?'

'Please dain't call him Thirsty. Mr Wilder and I christened him Thurston. His grendfather was *the* Thurston Wilder.'

I should have said, 'But Thirsty told me *he* was *the* Thurston Wilder. One of them is obviously an imposter.' Instead, being a coward at heart, I said in this really interested voice, 'Really?'

I switched off my brain for five minutes while she told me about the great Thurston Wilder, the actor.

'Gosh,' I lied. I wasn't really goshed at all. I'd heard this stuff a dozen times before. With a mother like this, no wonder the poor little nurd was hyper.

'Is that *Eshley*?' she asked hopefully. I shuddered. Nobody in his right mind would be Ashley if he didn't have to be. If I happened to be Ashley by some dreadful mistake, the first thing I would have done was get major plastic surgery on my face. Still, she obviously wanted me to be Ashley. Ashley's family have got a swimming-pool and Ashley is supposed to be a Good Influence. If they knew the sort of video-nasties he gets, they wouldn't think he was. Anyway, something told me that this wasn't the moment to be Ben so I said, 'Mmm-hmm' – which I thought was quite a good imitation of anybody except me.

'Oh, good,' she said. 'I'm *say*oo gled you called. Thurston had a veh, veh nasty accident yesterday – he's hurt his neck. I want him to hev a quiet day with no excitements. Could you arrange that, Ashley dear?'

I made a few Ashley-noises and heard T.W. being summoned to the phone.

'What do you *want*?' said the grandson of the great actor with his usual charm. 'I was trying to finish a computer program.'

It was time for my American accent. 'You're not impressin' me, yuh four-eyed phoney,' I said.

'Who is this?'

'Unless you want to have to stay in all day and play trains with Ashley, you'd better not get too clever with me, feller,' I said.

Thurston is quick, I'll give him that. He knew it was me but his mother was still in the background. He kept quiet so I knew I could afford to drop the accent and give him a hard time with a bit of British sarcasm. 'I hear our Thirsty Boy had a nasty accident. Does that mean he gets lots of love and *treats* out of that naughty little crick in the neck? Come on, what did you get?'

The silence was very tense, very interesting.

'Now, let me see . . . Did you get to stay up late and watch the Midnight Movie?'

'No,' said Thurston, grumpily.

'What, better than that? Not the compact disc player? They did, didn't they! They promised T.W. a CD player because he'd got a twist in his upper vertebral column! I don't believe it! Oh, well done, Thurston. Oh, I bet you had to do some acting for that. Your Grandaddy would have been so proud of you.'

'What exactly are you suggesting . . . Ashley. . . ?' Thurston said, carefully. I thought so. He *had* got himself into an awkward little spotty.

'And now Mummy thinks Thurston should rest and be ever so quiet and not go out this afternoon and play rough games with rough people like Ben. Right?

Well, that's a shame, 'cause Max and I are going out with Chris and Andy and Bruno and James and maybe Bruno's dad and a couple of other people. And we're going down to the field and we're going to try out Max's baseball gear. Like the idea?'

'Maybe,' said Thurston, grudgingly.

'Just maybe? Look, if Bruno's dad comes, maybe we'll have ourselves a hamburger and hotdog cookout in real Texan style. Yum yum. But, of course, with your bad neck, you'll probably be off your food. . . ?'

'Oh,' said Thurston. I knew that would get him. If Bruno's dad was coming, we were going to have a *gurrreat* time because he is a six-foot-ten Texan and he likes to carry kids about on his shoulders and he really knows all the rules of baseball and he loves hamburgers and Baskin Robbins ice-cream and he likes everyone else to like them, too.

'You'd like to come, wouldn't you? But you want your mumsie to think you're going to play with Ashley, don't you? This is going to cost you, Thurst, because I suspect you told your mummy that Ben had something to do with hurting your poor little neck . . .'

'No. I said it was Sniff.'

'Ah, blaming a poor defenceless woof-woof. Right Repeat after me . . .'

I did enjoy hearing Thurston admit that he was a

twisted four-eyed son of a two-toed knock-kneed wombat, even if it was only in a whisper . . .

★

. . . So anyway, there was Sniff, going round and round and collapsing and nibbling his paws and huffing and snarling and all that. I was just sitting on a deckchair on the patio thinking what a scatter-brained old bathmat he was, when I heard the unmistakable quick slapping of two small bare feet on the flagstones. Just for a moment, because she wasn't screaming, it crossed my mind that this might not be my nutty little sister, but a quick glance at the pink bottom and the fat little legs twinkling beneath a T-shirt that had raspberry yoghurt even round the back, was enough to confirm that this was indeed the slippery Sal. She was supposed to be having a nap after lunch. Mum and Dad were having a little zizz and Sally Shinybot was supposed to be having a little zizz too. *And* she was supposed to be wearing the nappy that she was now clutching and waving over her head. She had obviously just slipped it off like a bikini. Even from where I was sitting, one whiff was enough to tell you why she had decided to remove it.

Now the question was, what was she doing running into the garden waving a nappy over her head and making no noise *at all*?

Performing an innocent little dance?

No.

Hanging out her little wet nappy?

No.

Drying her twinkly little botty-boo?

Nope.

And did the doggy know what she was up to?

Alas, no. The doggy was so intent on nibbling his paws and going round and round, that he had the nappy over his head before he knew what had hit him.

In some ways, it was a bit surprising that Sniff didn't give Sal a good nip. He could have got away with it in any court. You can see the headlines: I WAS PROVOKED! SAYS DOG IN NAPPY ON THE HEAD CASE.

The truth is that he probably thought Sal wasn't a human at all but was some kind of freaky puppy. Besides, I think he quite likes having nappies on his head. He dashed round the garden for a bit looking

like a doggy Darth Vader. Sal and I were both in hysterics. Then he got the nappy off his head. But instead of running away and leaving it – which would have been understandable – he decided to take the game a stage further. He picked up the soggy thing in his teeth and charged Sal with it. She couldn't have screamed louder if I'd threatened her with the clothes-prop.

Round she went, like a wind-up toy with Sniff dancing behind, nudging and slapping at her with the wet nappy. That was OK. I had a good laugh about that. But then he stopped chasing Sal and charged over to where I was wallowing in my deckchair. He dashed up to the patio, put his front paws up on my knees and shook the nappy like a rat. A horrible spray formed in the air and fell like smelly rain. I was trapped, floundering and kicking and unable to get up.

Mum and Dad threw open their bedroom window to find out what the dickens all the racket was that had woken them from their beauty sleep, when the racket suddenly increased in volume: the deckchair had collapsed on my fingers and it didn't half hurt.

*

Thurston turned up at the field that afternoon looking a bit self-conscious in his neck-collar. It was one of those foam supports they give to hospital-cases

– people recovering from crashes, that sort of thing.

'Oh, dead trendy, Thurston,' I said. 'That's what they call a turtle-neck, is it?'

There were one or two mocking hoots from the middle-distance where Andy, Chris, James, Bruno and Max were taking it in turns to zap balls side-arm into the fat catcher's-mitt that Bruno's giant dad was demonstrating.

'Typical,' Thurston said, and then to me, 'Don't be so puerile.'

I was saved from having to reveal my ignorance about that one by the beefy voice of Bruno's dad. 'C'mon, you guys. Git over here real quick. We aim to have ourselves a game of baseball. Let's go!'

Bruno's dad, having entrusted the catcher's-mitt to Andy, was now standing with his massive legs plunked apart and a baseball bat held like a caveman's club over his shoulder. Then, holding the handle firmly in his left hand, he turned sideways-on to his son who was standing fifteen metres away, flipping the baseball from hand to hand, ready to pitch. Bruno's dad took one or two professional-looking practice-swings as he did so.

'Batter up, son!' he bawled.

Bruno took the peak of his baseball cap between his finger and thumb and swivelled it over his left ear. OK, that was cool. But you should have seen the way he swayed back, lifting his right knee high, and pumped that pill at his powerful poppa.

Wow! That ball was invisible. Max, who was playing backstop at what he thought was a very safe distance, threw himself to the ground with his hands on his head. There was no need though, 'cause with a resounding POP! Bruno's dad swung his club in a powerful arc and launched that ball towards some distant galaxy.

'All *rrright*!' yelled all the players, getting into the spirit of the thing. And then, even louder, when the ball materialized after its journey into space . . . 'YOURS!'

Surely it wasn't coming towards us!

'Yours! No, yours!' Thurston and I screamed at each other simultaneously.

'Get hold of it, you custard!' I shouted at Thurston, waving my bandaged fingers.

'Get hold of it yourself, you moron! My neck!' howled Thurston.

'My fingers!' I explained, waving them even more frantically.

'What's wrong with your fingers, you fake?' This coming from the guy who looked like an imitation of The Curse of the Mummy's Tomb just because of a little stiffness in the neck.

'Sniff did it!'

'That's it, blame it on the dog!'

'Well, I bet mine hurts more than yours.'

The truth was, I wouldn't have attempted to catch that ball if you'd paid me a zillion quid. It probably had ice on it. And now the afternoon was going to be ruined. Thurst and me were going to be branded as a couple of wimps who hadn't got the bottle to catch a baseball. How would we ever live it down?

And then, miraculously . . . *Whummmppp!!*

There was Sniff like the Caped Crusader, a blurred tangle of feet and fur. Sal's mad mongrel, the hero of the hour. We never heard him coming but here he was and never more welcome as he grabbed that ball with a SNAP! that would have knocked the teeth out of a lesser breed of beast.

What a leap! What a catch! What a hound!

'Yeah!' everyone shouted, thinking what a shame it was the television cameras weren't there to capture the moment.

'Wow!' boomed Bruno's dad, obviously impressed, and thundering over for a closer look. 'Whose is that dawg? He's *gotta* be in the team!'

'That's Sniff,' Thurston said. 'He's Ben's dog.' He obviously felt it was safe to say that seeing Sal was not around to dispute it.

'Well, are we gonna get our ball back, feller?' Bruno's dad said to Sniff. Sniff skipped away, growling happily through a mouthful of baseball.

'I'd be a bit careful if I were you,' Thurston warned the Jolly Giant. 'He can be dangerous, that dog. See what he did to me?' He pointed at his neck.

'And me,' I put in, holding up my hand. 'Practically amputated my fingers earlier on.'

'Izzat so?' drawled Bruno's dad. 'Well this here critter deserves ta be treated with some respect, huh?' He got down on his hands and knees. 'Jes the kinda dawg I admire. C'mon, feller. You wanna wrestle?' He pushed a meaty forearm in Sniff's direction.

Sniff didn't need another invitation. He dropped the ball and got in there, playfully locking his jaws on the offered arm and snarling mightily. This was the signal for everyone else to join in and seven kids, even one with his neck in a collar and one with bandaged fingers, piled on to the Man Mountain until he was weak with laughter.

'OK. That's it. I give in!' he panted from underneath a heap of battling boys and a frantic dog. Thurston got a bit carried away and caught him one under the chin with his knee, but even this didn't knock the fun out of it or the smile off Bruno's dad's face. If only more parents would let you beat them up.

'Man, am I hot!' said Bruno's dad, shedding boys like a good-humoured bucking bronco. 'What say we postpone this here baseball game for a little while? I could eat a quart of Baskin Robbins. Who wants a Rocky Road ice-cream?'

We were all on our feet in a flash! There were one or two votes for Blueberry and Bubblegum but no one was really fussy. Not as long as it was good stuff and plenty of it.

'What's that dog o'yours gonn' eat?'asked Bruno's dad as we all jogged in the direction of his red-painted Cherokee Chief Jeep. 'Tutti Frutti? He looks like a Tutti Frutti dawg.'

'Will they have any Nutty Casey?' Thurston panted. I thought that was quite funny, for him.

'Nutty Casey, eh? I *like* that!' boomed Bruno's dad. 'Double rations for the walking-wounded!'

'Does that include me?' I said, waving my bandaged fingers.

'Darn right it does, boy. Let's go!' We piled into the jeep.

As we ripped off down the road towards Baskin Robbins, Thurston let the wind get to his brain. 'I've changed my mind about the flavour I want,' he shrieked. 'I'm having Blackberry and Buffalo! No, no . . . I'm having Raspberry Rat Ripple. . . !'

I couldn't let him get away with it, could I? 'Thurston,' I said, 'how do you spell "puerile"?'

Sniff, the Lizard Man and Thurston's Secret

Three of us had crowded into a little hut on legs that was at the top end of Max's garden. It had once been a chicken hutch but most of the smell had gone and we'd swept it out with bunches of grass. If we sat with our backs to the walls and kept our knees up, there was just enough space for us all. The doors closed pretty tightly, so we could sit in the dark and talk. One or two beams of light got in through the cracks but not enough to spoil the atmosphere. It's interesting, the kind of talk you get in a dark place.

'What I sometimes do. . . !' said Max, his freckled face redder than ever in the light of the bicycle lamp that Thurston was shining into it, '. . . Thurston, pack it in! That's blinding, that is!'

'I'm just checking your eyes,' said Thurston. 'I wanted to see how fast your pupils dilate.'

'Yeah, well pack it in,' said Max.

Thurston lay the lamp on its back so that it shone on the wooden roof that was so low we had to bend our heads, even though we were sitting.

'What I sometimes do is, if I'm in the back of the car – and, you know, getting a bit bored – I wind down the window a bit. Then I look at the line on the top of the window and where the line touches the trees and lampposts going by, I chop them off . . . *fffss, fffss, fffss* . . . like that.' He showed us with the side of his hand.

'I do that!' said Thurston, banging his head on the roof. 'Well, sort of. What I do is, I get a bit of muck or a raindrop or something on the window and I get down low in the seat and – you know the way telephone wires seem to go up and down in waves? Well, I try and keep the raindrop or whatever on the top wire and I jump it over the telephone poles.'

I wanted to say how I'm always shooting down planes with little bits of muck on the window but Max was in quicker.

'D'you ever . . . when it's raining, right? Do you ever . . .'

'Race raindrops down the window? Yeah,' I said.

'No, I'm not talking about that. I'm talking about

windscreen wipers. Every time they go across and come to the end . . .'

'. . . Complete their arc,' said Thurston. Typical.

'Whatever,' said Max. 'Anyway, when they get to the end, do you ever try to get them to hit the trees and that?'

'A bit like that,' said Thurston. 'Only I try to miss.'

'Tell you what I do,' I said. 'When you're walking home. It's a bit dark, OK? So you hurry along because you're a fair way from home. I'm not saying that you're actually scared of getting mugged or anything, but you know. . . ?'

I could feel the hut rocking on its legs as the others nodded in agreement.

'OK, you want to get home as quickly as you can. You hear a car coming behind you and you see its lights. You don't turn round but you say to yourself, "If I can get to that gatepost before that car comes alongside me, I shall be all right." Ever done that?'

'Something like that,' said Max.

'Exactly. That's exactly what I do,' said Thurston.

'With me, it's . . .' Max was anxious to get it right. He was fed up with Thurston finding words for him. 'If I'm a bit worried about something – like exams or something like that, right? In our road, it's got paving stones on the path . . . yes? And then the grassy bit at the edge where the trees are. Remember?'

Thurston and I did remember.

Max went on. 'Say there's a stone, a pebble or something on the paving stones, right? So what I do, I give it a boot. I toe it . . .' Now the hutch was really rocking as Max tried to demonstrate.

'Hoy!' shouted Thurst and me together.

'Sorry. Anyway, I toe it and if it goes *straight* – keeps on the paving stones without hitting a wall or bouncing on to the grass or anything . . . that's it, then. I'm OK then, I'm going to pass my exams or whatever.'

'Tell you what I do sometimes if I have to get up in the middle of the night – you know – and pull the chain . . .' said Thurston.

'Surprised you can reach,' said Max.

'I shall ignore that,' said Thurst. 'No, when I pull the chain . . . I . . .' He hesitated.

'What?'

'Oh never mind.'

'No, come on, Thurston. What?'

'No, it's OK. Forget it. Doesn't matter.'

'*Thurston!* This is getting annoying.'

It was obvious that Thurston was about to reveal something really interesting about himself. He had let himself get carried away with all the talk about the weird things people do in their heads all the time. Now he didn't want to give away anything that Max and I could use against him.

'So. . . ? You're annoyed . . . who cares? That's just tough buttocks!' said Thurston, pushing open the door with his shoulder and swinging his legs out. The sudden rush of light was dazzling and Thurston was off, cackling with laughter before Max and I realized what was happening.

'What's "buttocks"?' said Max, in spite of himself, spilling out into the weeds and tall grass after him.

'Look it up,' called Thurston triumphantly, legging it as fast as he could down the garden to where Max's mum was hanging out washing and where he would be out of the firing-line.

It wasn't until much later that day that I was to find out what Thurston's secret was.

★

The afternoon looked as if it was going to be well boring. Dad had gone off to the breaker's yard to find a part for the car without waiting for me. While Sal had a zizz, Mum was sitting at the kitchen table, finishing some typing. I stood over her, watching the letters smack on to the paper and admiring the way she could manage to type without having all the little hammers bunching together like they do when I try it. As a matter of fact, it wasn't long before two of the hammers did stick together. Mum leant forward and pinged them apart and told me to buzz off.

'Now look what you've made me do,' she said. 'Leave me in peace for a bit.'

'I don't know why you don't learn to use the word processor,' I said. I knew that would annoy her because I'd heard her complaining to Dad that she wanted to go on a course to learn, but didn't have time because of me and Sal and Sniff and him and the house and her various jobs, etc, etc.

'You are such a pain, Ben,' she said, scraping back her chair. 'You're bored, aren't you? That's your trouble. Where's Thurston this afternoon?'

'Gone to the orthodontist to see about a brace.'

'Well, what about Max?'

'Shopping for shoes.'

'Right, my lad, I've got just the thing for you.'

I felt myself going limp.

'Deliver these for me.' She reached down a bunch of envelopes from the second shelf of the dresser, and seeing my droopy face, 'There's an ice-cream sundae in it for you.'

'Make it a cheeseburger with fries and a strawberry shake and you're on,' I said.

Was I going to get the sermon on junk food or was the possibility of peace and quiet going to swing it?

'OK. Compromise. You freak out on additives *if*, when she wakes up, you take Sal – and Sniff – with you.'

'Mum! You know they'll never let us in.'

'Where?'

'McDonald's.

'Well, you'll just have to ask someone to hold Sniff for you while you go in – or make two journeys.'

'That's not fair,' I said. 'Where do these have to be delivered, anyway?'

Mum gave me a quick run-down on the best route to take so that I could deliver the letters and end up at McDonald's without going over the same ground too often. Then she said, 'Now listen, Ben. This is important. When you deliver this one to Mr and Mrs Bell . . . Are you listening?'

I nodded but I wasn't really . . . at the time. If people tell me to pay attention, it's like pulling a plug out in my brain.

'When you deliver this one to Mr and Mrs Bell, *don't* let the man who lives next door see you delivering. We've had him at the club before and he's a heck of a nuisance. He eats all the biscuits and swears at the ladies. His name is Mr Brynmore and he lives at number 6, Radnor Road. Make sure that you don't attract his attention when you deliver to the Bells at number 4. You have got that straight, haven't you?'

I should have paid more attention, of course, but most of my attention was on burgers and fries and the rest of it was occupied with the thought that I'd better make a fuss about doing any of this, just to make sure that Mum would reckon she was getting value for money. 'Oh, Mum! That means I'll have to walk miles . . .'

At the mention of the word 'walk', Sniff arrived. When I say arrived, I mean *materialized*. Talk about 'Beam me up, Scotty.' That animal can be hundreds of metres away. He might have his head down a hole he's just scraped in the lawn. He might be sleeping under your duvet. But at the mention of the word 'walk', something happens to his molecules. For a micro second, he goes stiff, as though he's been freeze dried or electrocuted. His ears, his tail, his legs, his fur – everything shoots out in different directions like millions of automatic car aerials. Then he just throws himself into motion, going flat out, scrabbling like some nutty swimmer.

This time, as usual, we hadn't had time to figure out what the thunder on the stairs was before he was in the kitchen, his backside banging against the cupboards and his tail sweeping dangerously close to the cups and vases on the shelves. Before she could stop him, he had his paws on Mum's papers on the table. He scrunched and slid them about, and as Mum got her shoulder under him and heaved him off and on to the floor more papers flipped into the air.

Meanwhile, Mum's shouting had woken Sal from her nap and she bumped down the stairs on her bottom. She stood, looking wobbly and just-woken-up in the kitchen doorway with all her hair sticking out and her blanket held to her cheek. Sniff caught sight of this human bundle, and rushed to greet it just as Sal staggered sideways. For a second, it was a bit like a mini bullfight, until Sniff dived into the blanket and plunged on into the hall, sliding along the polished floor like a runaway sledge. Sal the matador, meanwhile, refused to let go and was dragged several metres after him until they both crashed into the hall table and sent the phone to the floor with a clatter and a jingle.

So the scene that Dad walked in on must have looked pretty bad. Anyway, he worked out what to do straight away. He thrust his hands into his jacket pocket, whacked a handful of coins into my hand and told me to get Sniff and Sal out of the house sharpish.

The first part of our journey that afternoon was pretty slow. Sal insisted on holding Sniff's lead *and* all the letters that Mum had asked me to deliver. Sniff was very interested in every tree, bush, lamp-post, telephone pole, cigarette packet, sweet paper, Coke tin, scrap of newspaper and in most blades of grass, and stopped to pee on every one of them. Whenever he stopped for a pee, he dragged the pushchair sideways. When the pram went seriously sideways, Sal dropped the letters and I had to stop. If I tried to take them away or to hold the lead, she screamed. Still, at least when we swerved to a halt and Sal dropped the letters, I had a chance to take a quick look at the addresses on the envelopes.

All the letters were addressed to old people. They're members of a group called The Ten-Thirty Club and they meet to have cups of tea and natter and to listen to very boring people giving them talks on how to knit egg-cosies and how to put flowers in a vase . . . that kind of stuff. Each envelope included a list of the dates for the next month's meetings and the topics for the talks.

The first house we had to deliver to was Mr and Mrs Raggs'. That was easy because their gate had broken, and I dragged Sal and Sniff up to their front door without much trouble. Sal watched closely as I pushed the letter through the letterbox.

'Me do dat,' she said.

'I've done that one. You do the next one.' Then I noticed that Sniff was squatting on the lawn, looking thoughtful, and I shouted 'No, Sniff!' but it was too late and Sniff was already scooping up great chunks of the lawn with his hind legs in an attempt at a cover-up.

We left there in a hurry.

At the next house, the Davidsons', Sniff went after their cat and I got pulled across a couple of flower-beds before I could get him under control. I turned round in time to see Sal pushing four or five envelopes through the letterbox. I was going to ring the bell and ask Mrs Davidson to let me have back the spares but I changed my mind because I didn't particularly want to have to explain about the flowers that weren't standing up any more.

So off we went to Myrtle Street, to the place where a lot of oldies live. It's a big, square building with a warden's flat. I knew that a couple of the Ten-Thirty ladies came from here but I hadn't exactly listened when Mum told me their names. I looked at the remaining envelopes. There were three of them. They were a bit sort of screwed up by now and the addresses, which Mum had written in ink, had got rather runny and smudged where Sal had been sucking them. I wondered whether some of the envelopes that Sal had posted through the Davidsons' letterbox ought to have been delivered to The Myrtles.

Now what? I looked again, trying to make sense of the names and addresses. Two of them, I was pretty sure, said 'The Myrtles' under the names. But what was this other one? Was it Mr Bridgeman, Brighouse, Blackmouse (didn't seem too likely) . . . Brynmore? That was it. Now, where did he live, then? It was no good. Sal's dribble had run most of the writing into a smeary mess. But I remembered, then, Mr Brynmore. There was something I had to remember about him. He lived somewhere in Radnor Road and . . . he would be very upset if I didn't invite him. Phew! Good thing it had come to me or Mum would have done her nut.

Congratulating myself on my excellent memory, I let Sal post the two letters for The Myrtles in the warden's letterbox and set off for Radnor Road to get rid of the last one.

We made very good progress now. Sniff seemed to have run out of wee (which was unusual for him; Dad says he has a bladder like a petrol tanker) and Sal was happily occupied chewing the corners off the last letter. We soon got to Radnor Road and came to two houses that shared the same drive. One half of the gate had 4 on it and the other had 6.

As I opened the half to number 4, an old lady and gent who looked quite pleased to see us came out of their front door and gave us a cheery wave. I was trying to wriggle Sal's pushchair through the gate when Sniff slipped his lead and went tearing up the drive towards the old couple, barking in his usual friendly way. Before he had a chance to give them a good lick and a sniff, they darted inside and slammed the door shut again.

Not so jolly and cheery after all. I was just thinking how weird some people can be, when the door to number 6 creaked open and a small, skinny, unshaven old bloke with squinty eyes and a droopy green cardigan, slid out on to the drive like some nasty green reptile out of its hole. In the middle of his bristly face, there was a crack for a mouth. Out of the crack, when it opened, came some disgusting words. I took a quick look at Sal to see if she had heard the words clearly. If she went home and tried them out on Mum and Dad, they were very likely to blame me for teaching them to her. She was interested in the old reptile all right, but I couldn't tell if she'd heard what he'd just said. *Anyway*, Sniff heard the words and he knew what they meant, because he did a U-turn in the drive and came clattering back to me and Sal with his tail between his legs. He was so upset, he even let me put his lead on without mucking about.

'What do you want, then?' rasped the Reptile.

'I dot a letter for you,' said Sal and held out the soggy chewed remains of the last of the letters.

'Well, bring it 'ere, then!' he croaked. 'You don't expect me ta come down the drive for summink I might not even want, do ya?'

I wasn't too keen on going up to him, I can tell you, but I went – licking my lips and trying to whistle. Sal and Sniff sat quietly and still by the gate as though they were under a spell or something. I put the letter into a hand that was as shockingly cold and clammy as a newt that's just come out from under a stone at the water's edge. He looked at me with dark, lizard eyes. If he had eyelids, I never saw them, because he didn't blink once. He didn't even give a nod of thanks, just took the letter and stood, softly opening and closing his crack of a mouth.

I turned away from him and heard my feet slapping down the alley between the houses. My feet went

LIZARD-MAN LIZARD-MAN LIZARD-MAN. I didn't turn round to look at him, I just swivelled Sal's pushchair round, picked up Sniff's lead and bumped out of the gate as quickly as I could. I knew he was still looking at us with those unblinking eyes when we hurried out of sight round the corner.

After that, we deserved a good blow-out and I think we all felt a bit more normal when we got McDonald's in our nostrils. Sniff and Sal perked up no end. I felt in my pocket as we reached the glass doors and was surprised to find such a lot of money. Not like Dad to throw money about usually – but there you are. He obviously wanted us to have a specially good time for being helpful.

I had a bit of trouble at first finding anyone to hold Sniff while Sal and I went in and ordered. In the end, this kid with pink hair and a lot of studs on his jacket said he'd do it for a couple of quid, so I thought – why not? He obviously had a bit of experience with dogs, because he managed to hang on to Sniff even though Sniff was dead keen to get into the restaurant and kept whining and scratching on the window. He gave me and Sal time to order Big Macs, large fries, cherry pies and strawberry shakes and a quarter pounder for Sniff. He likes them.

★

When I got home, Mum and Dad had a real go at me.

Never mind that I'd been trailing round the streets with Sniff and Sal and letting them have loads of peace and quiet. OK, Sal sicked up her cherry pie, but I got a lot of it off the pushchair and her clothes by the time we got home. It could have been a lot worse if I hadn't thought of eating most of her Big Mac and letting Sniff share her strawberry shake. We didn't get any thanks for that, though, and Dad said he hadn't meant to give me all that money and certainly hadn't expected me to spend it all. He was specially cheesed off about the dogsitter. Anyone would think it was *easy* to get someone to hold on to a dog like Sniff.

Mum was narked about these phone calls she'd been getting. Apparently the Raggs had rung to say that Sniff had excavated their lawn and done 'something unmentionable' in their garden. You would have thought they'd never seen one before in their lives. And the Davidsons. They'd rung to complain that I had vandalized their begonias and dumped a whole pile of letters on them that I was supposed to deliver myself. The warden from The Myrtles complained that she had received invitations to the Ten-Thirty Club for people who weren't living in her flats and Mr and Mrs Bell had rung and said that they hadn't got any letter and that I had set the dog on them.

What upset Mum most was a phone call from Mr

Brynmore to say that he was going to start coming to the club again and that he was going to bring his brother who was deaf.

'Who's Mr Brynmore?' I asked.

'That horrible man who swears at everybody! I especially asked you not to let him know we were planning more meetings.'

'What him? The Reptile? Oh Mum, I'm really sorry, but anyone can make a mistake,' I said.

*

It was an 'early bath' for me that night, as they say. In bed – well, in the bathroom, anyway – at the same time as Sal went up. Maybe that's why I woke up in the middle of the night to go to the loo.

It was really quiet as I crossed the landing. The one, weak little light made it a bit spooky, too. I heard my bare feet on the polished wooden floor going LIZARD-MAN LIZARD-MAN LIZARD-MAN LIZARD-MAN.

As soon as I has finished in the loo, I took a deep breath. I took a firm grip on the chain and gave it a quick yank downwards. Before the water stopped flushing, I sprinted across the landing, swerved round the corner, nipped along the passage, dodged into my room and dived into bed and under the duvet. I waited until I was breathing more steadily and the blood in my ears had stopped pounding, and risked a look out from under the covers. There was enough light from the landing to show that it was all right . . . no sign that anything had followed me . . . I was safe.

Then it hit me. Of course! I had to have a little chuckle . . . because I had suddenly worked out for myself what Thurston's best-kept secret was. 'Tough buttocks', eh? I'd give him *tough buttocks*! Boy, was he going to suffer when I told Max what a wimp he was.

Sniff Finds a Seagull

I was wondering how you say in French, 'The dog in our kitchen has got hazel-nut spread and feathers on.' I could do the first bit all right and I was just thinking to myself that there probably wasn't any French for the rest of it, when I heard Tom's mum scream. This was partly because there *was* a dog in the kitchen with hazel-nut spread and feathers on. I was watching him through my periscope, so I should know.

It was a good periscope . . . worked really well. I could see brilliantly into the kitchen from outside on the patio. OK, I could have just looked without using the periscope, but then I could have been seen from indoors. The whole point of a periscope is to look round corners or over things without being seen, so, as I say, this one was dead good. I'd been watching for about five minutes actually. I'd told Mum that I'd keep an eye on Sal and Tom in the garden while she and Bunty were upstairs, looking at this wardrobe Mum had just bought at an auction. They were trying to decide whether to strip it or stencil it. I would have chucked it out, but there you are. So I sat at the garden table on the patio and got on with finishing my periscope while Sal and Tom mucked about with a couple of Transformer toys that Tom had brought with him. Sniff had disappeared somewhere.

Sal and Tom enjoyed themselves in their little kiddie way for a bit. They bent the Transformers about and didn't seem to mind if they didn't quite turn into guns or robots. Then they ran up and down on the patio going, 'Do diss!' and 'Look at me!' and then Sal chucked her Transformer at Tom and said, 'I can frow diss?' Tom thought that was a good idea and threw his Transformer as far as he could off the patio on to the lawn. Sal picked hers up and did the same thing. Then they jumped down off the patio and picked up the Transformers and ran back up the two steps and chucked them off again.

The great thing was that while they were whizzing about, they didn't keep coming over to see what I was doing, so I could get on with making the periscope. I'd seen them making one on 'Blue Peter' but I reckoned I could improve on it by using masking tape instead of Sellotape and by fitting a little mechanism for altering the angles of the mirrors. I'd had a bit of trouble and several goes at getting the case just right but I cracked the problem just when I thought I was running out of breakfast cereal packets.

I'd just about got it finished when Sal and Tom got fed up with the garden and headed for the kitchen. Handy, because now I could test whether it really worked.

I knelt on the patio, under the window. I could hear cupboard doors being opened and closed. I guessed what was going on and I brought the periscope up to my eye to check my theory. Brilliant! I could see everything . . . and there was little Sal dragging a chair up under the cupboard where the jam's kept. She was after the hazel-nut spread. The conversation went something like this:

SAL: 'I like some haysnut sped. You like some haysnut sped, Tom?'

TOM: 'Nahh.'

SAL: 'It in nat cupboard.' (Climbs on chair.) 'I get some for you.'

TOM: 'Dome wannenny.'

SAL: 'Here it is. In nis cupboard. Want some? Snice.'

TOM: 'Nahh.'

SAL: (Climbing down with large tub.) 'Can you take da lid off, Tom? I can. Look. Dass easy.'

TOM: 'Wass dat?'

SAL: 'Dass haysnut sped. Dass nice. Here, open you mowff. Nice?'

TOM: '*Pppppthtppp.*'

SAL: 'Don't you like it? Snice.'

At that point, Sal dipped her fingers into the tub, put a handful of the gooey stuff into her own mouth and went '*Pppppthtppp*' because that's what Tom had done. Hazel-nut spread spattered over the nearby cupboard doors on to the floor. Then Tom dipped his fingers into the tub, scooped out some gunge and let Sal have another go. Sal took her turn to scoop some into Tom's mouth. This went on for a bit and then Sniff brought in the dead seagull.

He quite often brings in things if he finds them lying around . . . bones, shoes, sticks, old tennis balls, that sort of thing. He brought in a dried cow-pat once. He likes smelly things. I think that's why he brought in the seagull. Anyway, as soon as he saw the hazel-nut spread, he lost interest in the seagull and dropped it on the kitchen floor. And as soon as Sal and Tom saw the seagull, they lost interest in the hazel-nut spread. They changed places and started exploring.

Sniff didn't usually get a proper go at the hazel-nut spread and normally had to rely on licking Sal after she'd had some. So he was obviously very interested in the tub and got his head in as far as he could. Likewise, being too noisy and scary to get very close to a real live seagull, Sal and Tom must have thought that *they* were dead lucky to have a chance with this one that Sniff had found, especially as it didn't mind them having a close look at its feathers.

That was how there came to be such a lot of feathers and hazelnut spread on the floor and the cupboard doors and the dog and on Sal and Tom. And it wasn't long after that that Bunty came in and let out a scream that was surprising for a grown-up woman.

'Tommy! Sally! What an earth is going on?' she wailed. 'And oh, good grief! What is THAT!'

'It looks like a seagull,' said mum. 'And . . . Err!' she clamped her hanky to her nose. 'It smells as if it's been dead for a week.'

Sniff thought he was being congratulated for bringing in something really ace. Wagging the old tail into a fan that wafted a feathery cloud into the air, he darted forward and grabbed the seagull, growling playfully. He jumped up at Mum, planting his sticky great paws on her skirt and his sticky great face in her chest and offering her his prize.

'Get down, Sniff! Sniff, down! No, I don't want that. No!'

'Me have it,' said Sal, stepping forward.

Bunty grabbed her and hauled her up into the air as if she was snatching her from a minefield. Naturally, quite a bit of what had been sticking to Sal transferred to Tom's mum.

Meanwhile, my mum had got the back door open and was pointing outwards towards the distant horizon, calling 'Out! Out!' When that didn't work she got the mop out and half-scooped half-pushed Sniff into the garden and slammed the door after him.

Sal and Tom squealed furiously. I don't think they were shocked at the treatment Sniff had received from Mum. Actually, they were cheesed off that he'd pinched the seagull they'd been stopped from playing with. Now he was galloping off, down to the field to bury it somewhere near where he'd found it. As I watching him pounding off through the hole in the fence at the bottom of the garden, leaving a few white feathers stuck to the fencing boards on either side of the gap, I wondered what a stranger might think as they saw him galumphing along, fur and feathers waving together in the breeze. Headline: BIRDBEAST CAUSES RIOT ON RECREATION FIELD – TOWNSFOLK FLEE.

'Where's Ben?' said Mum in a voice that got Sal's attention and mine, even though I was outside.

'In da garding.'

'Stupid boy! What's he doing out there? He is supposed to be keeping an eye on you two little terrors! Now look at you. And this place. And me!'

'And me!' added Bunty. 'I am covered in gunk! What is this stuff?'

'Haysnut sped,' said Tom, who now knew. 'Snice.'

'And fevvers,' added Sal.

'I don't know about hazel-nut – but it certainly does spread,' said Bunty. (Dead witty.) 'It's spread all over this kitchen. How could two little kids make a mess like this in five minutes?'

'Not me and Tom,' said Sal, shaking her head seriously. 'Niff done dat.'

'Nahh,' agreed Tom, who meant 'yeah' but didn't like saying it.

'And I know just the person to clean it all up,' said Mum 'Ben!'

It was no good me explaining that I *was* keeping an eye on them. Never mind that I didn't take my eye off them. That didn't seem to count. No. I am irresponsible. I am a pain. I have no consideration for others. And I can blinking well clear up the whole sticky, revolting mess. And if I think I'm going out enjoying myself that afternoon, I've got another think coming. All that.

Took me ages to get that place cleaned up. *And* I had to wipe up stuff that wasn't even feathers or hazel-nut spread.

It wasn't until Dad came in hours later that anyone showed the least bit of interest in my periscope, either. He thought it was great – and might come in handy for finding things that had rolled under washing machines and sideboards and stuff like that. I think what really finished Mum off was that I'd cut up all the cereal boxes to make the case, so that the raisin bran and the muesli and the Shreddies and the Wheatoes all got mixed up together in the cake tin I tipped them in. That's the trouble with this country, not enough people appreciate the scientific spirit. It could be a genius staring them in the face – and all they can see are a few seagull feathers, a mucked-about muesli and a splash or two of hazel-nut spread.

Still, I must say we all had a laugh later on when Sniff came creeping back for his supper and we pounced on him and gave him a bath. But that's another story.

A School Visit for Sniff

Max was trying to persuade us that his granny had had both her legs turned round the wrong way in an accident on a paddle steamer.

We were between Maths and French. There was always a long wait between Maths and French because Monsieur Olivier had to come from right over the other side of the main school building and across the lawns to the two adjoining First Form rooms. We were in the one furthest away from the main school. It was hot in the classroom. The air was like bathwater and bad feelings were floating about in it. Beggs, who was normally a quiet kid, had got himself into trouble in Maths by dazzling Mr King with the inside of the tin lid of his geometry set. He was now recovering, trying to shade his tearful red eyes with one hand while the other was busy stabbing holes in the cover of his Maths text book with a pair of compasses. Rishi Das was asking for it, flitting about flicking people's ears. Max's freckles had gone sort of luminous and sweatbeads flickered on his face with the effort of trying to persuade me and Thurston that it was true about his granny.

'Where was this paddle steamer?' sneered Thurston. 'On the Mississippi?'

'Southend,' said Max. 'They used to have a paddle steamer went between Southend and Margate.'

'Rubbish!' I said, although I was quite interested. I was wondering how they got her on the stretcher. Did they lie her down on her stomach with her feet pointing up or put her on her back with her toes aiming at the deck? I wasn't going to give Max the satisfaction of asking him, though. 'You *can't* turn both legs round the wrong way.'

'The worst thing that happened to me,' said Thurston, ignoring Max's attempt to shout me down, 'was when I swallowed one of my contact lenses.'

'Come off it!' said Max. 'They don't let kids have contact lenses. You've always had glasses.'

Thurston removed his gogs and gave them a wipe with a special cloth that he kept for the purpose in his briefcase. 'I was a special case, actually. The Oculist . . .'

'Optician, it is,' corrected Max.

'The oculist,' Thurston continued, in an embarrassingly loud and piercing voice, 'told me that he felt I was mature enough to wear contact lenses.'

'Yeah, dead mature,' sneered Max who didn't want to push the optician business any further. 'So how come you swallowed one?' A pretty nifty one, that, for Max. He was pleased with himself and swung back in his chair to rest his elbow on Thurston's table. 'Eh, Thurston?!'

All Thurston had to do was to sit up quickly and take his weight off the table so that leaning Max sent it sliding backwards. Max crashed with his toppling chair to the floor.

Results: One broken chair. One very peeved Max. One very loud sarcastic groan from everyone in the form. One schoolbag (Thurston's) chucked across the room by Max. One extra-loud howl of rage from Hart. (Hart whacked by flying bag.) Loud crash as Wallace was smashed into the lockers by Hart who was trying to get past to thump Max. Angry shout from Wallace and loud squeal from Rishi Das who had finally got thumped for flicking Munford's ears.

Enter Monsieur Olivier. And it was 'Bonjour, la classe. Silence, la classe. Detention, la classe.'

'But, sir!'

'Not fair, sir!'

'I wasn't doing anything, sir!'

'Nor was I, sir!'

'It was them lot, sir!'

Monsieur Olivier put his hand into his case and took out a hammer. He brought it down with a splintering smack on the teacher's desk. Everyone jumped about six feet into the air, including Rickie Lomax whose mum had insisted that he sat in the front because he was a bit deaf. Poor old Rickie looked as though he was about to have a heart attack.

'May I av your attention, pliz?' said Monsieur Olivier who had already got it. 'Ziss is *un marteau*. Qu'est-ce que c'est?'

(Chorus.) 'C'est un marteau, monsieur.'

'Bon. We understond wan annozzer. Seat!!'

We did 'understond'. We all sat down and looked at the hammer, wondering what this nutty little teacher was going to do with it next.

'And now,' said Monsieur Olivier, putting away his little surpriser and pulling himself to his full five-feet-two-and-a-half inches, 'we continue wizz French.'

He picked up an exercise book, holding it between his finger and thumb as though it was a wet nappy or something. I recognized the drawing of a Slimeswine being zapped on the front cover of the book: it was mine.

'As everybuddy knows, the gutters of Paris are running wizz ze blood of small boys who do not remember to make agree all ze nouns and adjectives, oui?'

'Oui, Monsieur!' (This reply came from Rickie Lomax who was still shaking because of the hammer.)

'Therefore, we av *le petit chien* . . . which means, Wallace?'

'The small or little dog, sir,' said Wallace quickly.

'Keep eet seemple, Wallace. We don't want to confuse some of ze morons in ziss class, do we? We shall just say "ze leetle dog." But when we av ze plural – ze leetle dogs – zen, we av *les petits chiens*. Good . . . So why, BEN MOORE!. . .' (My turn to have a heart attack.) 'Why do we not remember to write . . .' He turned to the board and scribbled:

LES PETIT<u>ES</u> MAISON<u>S</u>

He underlined the ES on the end of PETITES and the S on the end of MAISONS and then put rings round them.

'I forgot, sir,' I said.

'Pipple who forget ziss are . . . WHAT ARE ZEY, BEN MOORE?'

'Verys wickeds boys?' I suggested.'

The sun glinted on one of Monieur Olivier's eyeteeth as he pulled his face into a very unfriendly grin. 'My mickey has been taken, eh? Very well. A leetle suffering for you and for all zoze who find eet funny. DOUBLE-DETENTION FOR ZISS CLASS! Any questions? Good. We will now do some work!'

*

It didn't get any cooler that day. The soggy air of the classroom was suffocating. I had received several messages. One was on a piece of paper that was so grey it could only have been through Begg's hands. It read, 'YOU DYE AFTER SCHOOHL.' It had to be Beggs who had written it because the only other dyslexic kid in the class was Rickie Lomax who was too skinny to risk being caught threatening anyone. Hardly a minute went by without somebody mouthing something nasty at me.

Quite apart from getting the detention, what was making people specially fed up was that almost everybody had made plans to go swimming. A lot of kids had talked about going to the Civic Centre to the open air pool – and there aren't that many days in the year when you can do that without going blue. Max and Thurston and I had been invited to Ashley's to swim in his own private pool. Big deal, but on a day like this, even if it meant sucking up to the world's most boring thicko, it was worth it just to float about in some cool, uncrowded water.

The idea came to me during English, the last lesson of the day. The thing about English with me is that I can do it and not have to worry about it. It's not like French where there are sneaky endings that you're not expecting and lists of weird words to remember. So while I was working through some dead easy comprehension questions, I was also thinking about

Monsieur Olivier's face. What I'd noticed about his face was that it was usually very, very red – as though his collar was too tight, or he was trying to keep quiet about the fact that a bus has just run over his foot. It was red most of the time, but once, I remembered, just once, I'd seen him go distinctly yellow. He was in the playground, having a chat with a bunch of teachers and laughing and joking about something. A minute or two later, Mrs Beam, the Head's wife, turned up with her Pekinese doggy under her arm and then . . . suddenly, that was it! Monsieur Olivier had stopped laughing and joking. He just stood there, completely frozen and pale and *totally terrified* . . .

I put my hand up.

'What is it, Ben?' asked Mr Clegg. 'Finished already?'

'Yes, sir,' I said. 'Do you mind if I make a quick phone call home, sir? I've got to make a few arrangements for after school.'

Mr Clegg had obviously heard about the class detention but since I caused him no trouble and did my English quickly and quite well, he couldn't see any reason to be awkward.

'Seems sensible to me, Ben,' he grinned. 'Off you go.'

As I went past the teacher's desk, he whispered,

'Not calling an ambulance, are you, son?' Good old Cleggy, he knew I was in a tight spot.

'Just phoning home, sir,' I said. 'Shan't be a sec.' I dashed out into the sunlight crunching along the gravel path. I felt twenty-four pairs of eyes on me as I jogged past the windows of my class and another twenty-five on me as I continued past the windows of the other First Form room next door. It only took me about ten seconds to get to the main building but I was in a terrible sweat by the time I got to the phone outside the Monitors' room. Two minutes later I was back at my desk, copying up a first draft of an essay about a nightmare and trying to work out the chances of my little wheeze coming off. I ignored Munford who whispered, 'Ringing mumsie to come and collect you, eh? You're not getting out of it like that, Bennie Boy.'

When the bell went, some of the kids next door came and made faces and signs at us prisoners before they nipped off across the lawns towards the junior gate. Quite a number of them had rolled-up towels under their arms and were obviously going straight to the swimming-pool.

That stirred everybody up even more, of course. They'd forgotten by now that I had nothing to do with the first detention, and I was getting a bad time being pushed and shoved about, when Monsieur Olivier came out of the door of the main building.

Straight away, every kid was sitting in his seat, trying to look angelic.

All the windows were open and we could hear Monsieur Olivier's feet on the gravel . . . *splash-splash, splash-splash, splash-splash*. We all had our backs to him but I sneaked a look and saw . . . oh, no! He was carrying a *huge* pile of marking. That was terrible; it meant that, even with good behaviour, we weren't going to get out of there before five o'clock at the earliest. Those firm footsteps meant nobody messes about with Monsieur Olivier. He was getting very close to the outer door. Twenty metres to go. I uncrossed my fingers, thinking that it was a complete waste of effort to cross them, when suddenly there was another sound, more distant than the splash-splash of furious French feet on gravel, but growing louder by the second. It was a *shuckatta – shuckatta – shuckatta – shuckatta* . . . Yes! He'd made it! It was the unmistakable lolloping gallop of the great hairy Beasty Boy. And in the nick of time, as they say. It was Sniff. None other.

As Monsieur Olivier came level with the window, Sniff crashed past him and pounded his loud paws on the outer door of the classroom. Monsieur Olivier's feet had stopped splash-splashing. In fact, he had stopped moving at all. There was no sign of him breathing, and he had gone the colour of cheese. For all you could tell, he had entered The Zone of the

Living Dead, except that the pouch under one of his eyes was twitching.

Sniff sat on the step outside and panted. He looked at Monsieur Olivier. He probably hadn't realized before that he was there – but since he couldn't get through the outer door without a little human help, he got off the step and lay down on the lawn to let Monsieur Olivier past. Sweat fell like raindrops down Monsieur Olivier's pale face and when Sniff went 'RRRALPH!' just once, a shockwave ran through his body that sent quite a number of the books and papers he was clutching pattering to the ground.

'Hang on, sir,' I called through the window. 'I'll give you a hand, shall I?'

Monsieur Olivier's only move was to raise his top

lip enough to show his eye-tooth. I knew that I was meant to take this as a smile meaning yes, but I couldn't help remembering that the last time I'd seen that eye-tooth, it was just before the announcement of a double detention. So I let him stand motionless in the afternoon sun, dripping sweat on to the gravel for a little bit longer before I repeated, 'Shall I, sir?'

'Yes . . . er . . . Ben . . . by all means. I av too many,' he said, like a ventriloquist, without moving his lips at all. 'Ben' came out 'Gen' and 'by' as 'guy'.

When I opened the outer door, Sniff came charging into the entrance lobby, tail wagging like mad. I ducked back inside, slammed the outer door while I nipped in and back to my place by the window.

'Sir,' I said. 'There's a huge dog. I've got him in the lobby. Did you see him?'

'Oh, really?' said Monsieur Olivier whose voice had gone up an octave. 'I did not notice heem. I was concentrated upon zees books, you see. I av so many, I drop zem.' He began to pick them up. He seemed in a great hurry all of a sudden.

'What shall we do about him, sir?' I said. 'He looks a bit . . . you know, sort of wild.' Sniff began to whine and scrape. He always does that when he wants to go out but it sounded now as if he might eat his way through the door if someone didn't open it for him.

'You must let heem calm down for a beet. He ees ot, no doubt.'

'Shall I let him out, sir?' I said.

'Non, non. Not yet.' (Nice bit of panic there.) 'Better not disturb heem. Wait a few minutes, I zinc. I av come to tell you only zat . . . er . . . ze detention is not necessary on an afternoon like zees. Not necessary at all. Zat is what I am ear for. I am departing now and er . . . when ze dog is calm, you can go also.' One more quick flash of the eye-tooth and he was off across the lawns and diving into the door of the main building.

As soon as he disappeared, a great cheer went up.

'What a bit of luck, that dog turning up,' said Munford, peering through the glass at Sniff. He jumped back as Sniff hurled himself at the door. 'But I don't fancy going out through that lobby. I'm cutting through the other classroom.'

'Me too,' said Rishi Das, grabbing his bag and diving out through the connecting door. Soon everybody had disappeared that way except me and Thurston and Max. I let Sniff in and he barged down the aisles, banging chairs and desks with his mad backside.

We took him along to the water fountain. Thurston pressed the button while I made a cup out of my hands and Sniff slurped thirstily.

'How'd you fix it?' asked Max.

'I knew Sal would be sitting there watching 'Henry's Cat' or something, so I phoned and I said . . . 'Listen, Sal, whatever you do, *don't* go to the side door and hold it open and say to Sniff "Go and find Ben".' That's all there was to it. Wicked, eh?'

'What's your mum going to say when she finds out?' said Thurston.

'Yeah,' said Max. 'She'll probably go mad.'

'I wouldn't be surprised,' I said, 'if she got so worked up, her legs went right round the wrong way. Then she'd have to ring up your granny to find out what to do about it.'

'My granny's in Wales,' said Max.

'Ah, but Mum could still ring her up,' I said.

'No, she couldn't!' said Max.

'Why not?'

'She's dead, that's why.'

'Bound to be, isn't she?' said Thurston. 'If she never looked where she was going. Probably walked under a steam-roller or something.'

'RRRALPH!' said Sniff, and there was no answer to that.

We all had our swimming trunks, so Max and Thurston whizzed home with me to drop off Sniff before we headed off for Ashley's pool. I was a bit worried about whether Mum had twigged what happened, but she wasn't there. She'd left a note saying that she'd taken Sal round to play with Tom and asking me to see if I could find Sniff who had disappeared. '*Sal has been v. naughty this aft*,' the note went on. '*She put the phone down before I could get to it and I THINK she might have let Sniff out. Enjoy your swim. Love, Mum.*'

We left Sniff in a nice cool spot round by the back of the garage with a few extra doggie biscuits than usual to chew. I closed the front door softly so not to disturb him and tiptoed down the front path with the lads.

'So you're going to let your little sister take the rap, are you?' teased Thurston.

'Course he is,' said Max. 'Let sleeping dogs lie, that's his motto.'

'Ha ha, very funny,' I said, breaking into a trot. 'You two had better be careful in Ashley's pool. There might be a paddle steamer with a cargo of contact lenses chuffing up and down. Could be dangerous.'

I must have covered about eighty metres before Max managed to catch me a stinger on the backside with a flick of his towel.

Sniff and the Well-Known Fact

It was a pity we couldn't find anything better to eat the popcorn to than some 'Lassie' programme, and it was a shame we didn't keep the volume down a bit.

It was great at first. Bruno had brought round to our house this huge carton of popcorn and a pint of butterscotch sauce. Bruno is a true son of his father, a Texan, who really knows how to eat. He is the junior version of his dad, Bruno W. Oakley Senior, the Jolly Giant, the Man Mountain, the man who goes for Baskin Robbins Rocky Road flavour ice-cream by the quart. Even if you never looked up in the air, and the only place you ever looked in your life was at the ground, you could tell that he was Bruno W. Oakley Senior's son. All you would have to do would be to look at his feet. They are *mega*. His dad's are even more mega – they're scary. In fact, when the Giant is off on business somewhere, all Bruno's mum has to do is put a spare pair of his shoes outside the door of their flat and it's better than having a burglar alarm.

So there were three pairs of feet on the coffee table, one of which was ginormous. The telly was on and everything was great, even if the only thing half way worth watching was a 'Lassie' film. Bruno, Thurston and me; there we were, sitting on our sofa, dipping into a carton like a bucket. This carton was so huge that you could take a handful and it didn't make any difference, and the popcorn was *beautiful*. It was the kind that squeaks and grumbles when you chew it . . . that was the dry part. And then every now and then, there would be a thick glob of butterscotch sauce that just slammed into your tastebuds as you churned the mixture up. It was *something else*, I'm telling you.

You couldn't hear anything for some time but popcorn exploding in your head, but then . . . somebody was dragging this little kid into a car. It was a kidnap. She screamed out 'Lassie! Lassie!' A big hand went over her mouth. Lassie'd never hear her now. There was a horrible silence. I was looking at the telly but swivelling my eyes round to look at Thurston and Bruno. Thurston was frozen, with a full fist held up to his open mouth, and Bruno's jaws, which up to now had been grinding away, were dead still. The butterscotch sauce ring round his mouth puckered.

The car tyres ripped up the dust as the crooks made their getaway. Where was that dog. . . ?

BLAM! The sitting room door smashed back against the sideboard. A thunder of hairy hooves and of a tail whacking the furniture. *Eeeeeeeee!* a sound almost too painful for the human ear. Forget Lassie – Sniff and Sal had arrived.

Bruno is quick for a big guy, but this time not quite quick enough. In a flash, he was standing on the sofa with the carton held aloft in his upstretched arm, doing an imitation of the Statue of Liberty. But Sniff was up on the sofa with him, jumping over Thurston and me and pounding on Bruno with his paws as though he was shaking fruit out of a tree. It worked. I didn't dare think about what was happening to the springs that were groaning under the weight of Bruno and his size 99s, but anyway, Bruno was shimmying about on the sofa, trying to keep his balance and save the popcorn. And while he was shimmying, popcorn was showering down.

'Hey!'

'Watch it!'

'Oof!'

'Down, boy. Geddoff!'

'You're spilling it!'

'What dat?' asked Sal, but she didn't hang around to find out. She saw that Sniff was going at the scattered popcorn like a cross between a chicken and a

Hoover. She grabbed him by the hair sprouting out of the back of his pecking head and heaved him aside so that she could get in there and taste some.

'Snice,' she told us, ignoring the fact that there was a fair amount of carpet fluff and dog hair mixed up with the popcorn and butterscotch. Then she was down on the carpet again, scrabbling for more and snatching what she could before Sniff recovered sufficiently from his scalping to risk getting back into the competition.

'Sal, get Sniff out of here!' I yelled. 'We're trying to watch an important film.'

'Gimme somma dat,' she said to Bruno, pointing at the carton he was cuddling like a baby. 'I want summa dat!'

'OK, well git that dawg outa here!'

But Sal had spied yet more popcorn and immediately thrust her hand down the back of the cushions on the sofa. With this hand she fisted some into her mouth, while she held the other one out, tightly closed, and shouted – spraying chewed stuff everywhere – 'Sit!' At that moment, all the spring went out of Sniff and he sat, quivering slightly, his head on one side and his eyes fixed on Sal's hand. Sal had got him under her spell and made the most of it. She got him to sit alongside the telly, cocking his head from side to side. It was as if he had a marble in his head and he wanted to stop it rolling out of either of his ears. Long strings of drool hung down from the corners of his mouth. And then very slowly, between finger and thumb, Sal delivered one tiny fragment of popcorn that he took with a wet *Schllop*. He churned it about hopefully for a second or two and then started rolling the old marble about again.

This was better than 'Lassie' actually, so Bruno, Thurst and I sat down on the sofa, flicking the odd glob of butterscotch popcorn at Sniff and half paying attention to the flickering screen. Lassie was now pawing at the ground outside the barn on this spooky old ranch. She started to scrape at the earth with her front paws and then to whine. It was as though Lassie had tugged at a piece of string with Sniff's nose on the end because, at the first hint of a whimper, his head jerked round and thunked against the screen.

'Hey! Get out of the way!' we all yelled, and Sal had the bright idea of throwing a handful of popcorn at his head. Some of it stuck to the fur round his ears, some of it went over his back, and some just pattered to the floor underneath him. Sniff went into a backward somersault, snapping like a crocodile and splashing drool everywhere as he flipped and knocked the telly sideways.

'Yuck!' yelled Thurston. 'He's spitting every where!'

'Hey!' bawled Bruno, 'I missed seeing what Lassie dug up!'

'Forget it,' I said. 'Let's get out of here.' We pounded up the stairs to my room.

'Now what are we going to do?' moaned Thurston.

'Finish off the popcorn for a start,' I told him, and we settled down, sitting on my bed, to the serious business of polishing it off before Sal and Sniff arrived. A couple of closed doors wouldn't hold those two for long.

In the time it took for Sal and Sniff to make enough

noise to get Mum in from the garden and up the stairs to tell me to stop teasing and not to be so mean and to share some popcorn with Sal, we had stuffed what was left of it into our mouths and chucked the carton into the waste-paper basket.

'Mum, she's such a pain! She ate most of it anyway and Sniff came in and mucked up our programme.'

It's true, Mrs Moore,' said Thurston in his Impress-a-Parent voice. 'Under the circumstances, we couldn't have acted with more generosity or restraint.'

'You said it, Thirsty,' Bruno said, admiring Thurston's smooth talk.

'Well I think you're a crowd of stinkers and a shower of greedy male chauvinist pigs,' said Mum, raising her voice above the sobs and howls of rage that were echoing up the stairs from below. She slammed the door, pounded downstairs and we heard her soothing Sal with offers of hazel-nut spread on crispbread.

'Phewie!' said Bruno. 'Your momma sure knows how to git riled.'

'It's her instinct, that is,' I explained. 'She's all right most of the time but when somebody threatens her infant,' (Miss Salt's biology lesson was coming back to me) out comes the protective behaviour, see? That's a well-known fact.'

As soon as the words were out of my mouth I

started blushing. Hot blood was pulsing in my checks and ears. I tried to cover up. 'Seen this?' I asked Bruno. 'It's a Flying Fortress. Dad picked it up for me at the jumble . . .'

'That reminds me!' Thurston had twigged. 'Talking of well-known facts . . . What did the bloke at the Boxing Board of Controls say?'

'Er, I haven't heard anything yet,' I lied. 'Hang on a tick, I'm just going for a pee.' I opened my door and nipped out on to the landing. Tripped out would be nearer the truth, actually, because Sniff was lying outside like a draught excluder. As I bolted for the loo, he barged into my bedroom.

I clicked the lock, pulled the seat cover down, and sat. I needed time to think. How was I going to get out of this one? I'd really let myself in for it by agreeing to write that letter.

*

What had happened was this. About three weeks before, Bruno, Thurst and I had been round at Thurston's, mucking around in his shed. He was showing us this device he was working on that would interfere with all the television sets within a hundred metres' radius. That only meant about six or seven houses, because Thurston's dad's an estate agent and they live in this fairly flash house. He wanted to annoy his neighbours because a number of them had objected to his parents about us all riding our bikes up and down their private road and doing wheelies in their driveways. He had almost finished building the Interferer, but during a test-run, he had overloaded the circuit and burnt out a couple of resistors. You could still smell them.

'You want to watch it, Thurston,' I said. 'You could easily start a fire like that.'

'Don't worry,' he said, cheerfully. 'I've rigged up an intermediate circuit-breaker. No problem.' I wasn't really convinced, but he went on, 'Tell you what really *is* dangerous . . . rice.'

'Here we go,' said Bruno, wearily. 'Another of Thirsty's Well-Known Facts.'

'My idea of a well-known fact is that Quentin Court is a school for rich thickos,' I said.

'It's gotta be,' agreed Bruno, 'if Ashley goes there.'

Thurston was not going to be put off by sarcasm. According to him, it was a well-known fact that rice is one of the most dangerous cargoes in the world. OK, we said. So what about H-bombs, petrol, nitroglycerine, liquid manure, etc, etc. . . ? Yes, but apart from obvious ones like that, he said, rice is *well-known* to be mega-dangerous.

Right, we went. So what kind of cargo were we talking about? Did he mean in planes? Even Bruno and I could work out that if you try to stuff a billion tons of rice into the hold of even a Jumbo Jet, that can be dangerous. You had to watch it with Thurston for that kind of tricky thinking. No, he didn't mean on planes or lorries or camels or donkeys or anything that could be squashed if you dropped a billion tons of rice on them from the top of Telecom Tower.

'I'm just talking about ships,' Thurston said. 'Rice is a really dangerous cargo on ships . . . and I'm not talking about overloading or anything like that. It's just dangerous and that's a well-known fact.'

'Who says?' This was Bruno jumping in with both his big feet. 'Who says this is a well-known fact?'

This is just the kind of tussle Thurston likes, because he's nippy and sneaky. He put his screw-driver down on the bench and looked at us both as if we were total wallies. 'Everybody! *And* . . .' (His piercing voice cut through everybody's jeers) 'I heard this play on the radio called "The Rice Ship" so that proves it.'

'OK, wise guy, what makes it so dangerous?' Bruno had never listened to a play on the radio in his life, so Thurston had got him sussed. As far as he was concerned, radio plays were what you launch into deep space to give the aliens some idea of what life used to be like on earth hundreds of years ago. No way could he win an argument like this with Thurston, no matter how huge his feet.

'OK. This is how.' (Thurston is sickening when he's like this.) 'You're sailing along in this cargo ship, right? You've got a load of rice on board. It starts to rain and the sailors start battening down the hatches, covering up the cargo. Now, one of the sailors is a complete incompetent . . . that's a bit of a nerd to you two morons. He can't be bothered to batten everything down properly and what happens? *One drop* . . . that's all it takes. One drop of water and one grain of rice starts to swell and then the next and the next and then BLAM! the cargo has swollen to ten times its original size and the ship goes bang like a balloon.'

'I've never heard of that happening,' I said.

'Happens all the time,' said Thurston, his wincy little eyes rolling about under his designer-gogs. 'Well-known fact.'

'I betcha Mexican jumpin' beans are whole lot more dangerous than just an old cargo of rice,' drawls Bruno. 'Mosta the time they're all gonna be jumpin' and hoppin' every which way, but *one time* they gonna jump together. And I'm tellin' you guys, if those there jumpin' beans all take a jump together *downwards* . . . that's so long old cargo ship. You ain't gonna find a whole lotta sea captains ready to sail with Mexican jumpin' beans, thats fer sure.'

'Pretty improbable,' Thurston said.

Still, old Bruno looked pretty pleased with himself, so I thought I'd better come up with a well-known fact of my own. The only one I could think of off-hand was the one about the boxer who got counted out while he was standing on his head.

'What are you talking about?' said Thurston.

'I'm telling you, Thurston, there was this bloke. He was in the ring, boxing away, and they got to about twelfth round, and they were both pretty whacked out, and this other bloke caught him one . . . WHAM! . . . like that. Sort of an uppercut, I s'pose. So he went over, sort of cartwheeled over into the ropes. Anyway, he finished up standing on his head, with his legs up in the air . . . *on his head*. And they counted him out like that.'

'That is impossible,' said Thurston, 'That is a load of old rubbish.'

Bruno didn't say anything. He just grabbed hold of me round the waist, yanked me off the wooden floor of the shed, banged the door open with his backside, turned me upside down and plunked me down on my head on the grass. It hurt. He let go of my legs and I fell flat on my back. That hurt too.

'There ya go, motormouth,' said Bruno. 'There's no way any guy's ever gonna just stand on his head if he's unconscious for ten seconds. No way.'

'It's a fact,' I insisted, giving my head a soothing rub. 'I can prove it. Anyone who knows anything about boxing knows about it. And anyway, you know how when you're dead you go all stiff, right?'

'So?'

'That's what they call rigor mortis. OK, well, when you're unconscious, sometimes you get this kind of temporary rigor mortis. That's what happened to this bloke.'

'How're you going to prove it?'

'Write to some Boxing Association, I s'pose,' I said.

'You want the British Boxing Board of Controls.' This was from Thurston. Who else?

They both stood over me while I wrote the letter. We got the phone number through Directory Enquiries for London, because it seemed pretty likely that it was going to be there somewhere, and we got the address from the lady on the switchboard.

After that, they walked down the road to the post office with me just to make sure I posted it off to 70 Vauxhall Bridge Road, London SW1V 2RP.

*

I pulled the chain. No way I could stay in the loo any longer without rousing even more suspicion. I realized that I'd been sussed as I crossed the landing, because it was so quiet in my room. I put my ear to the door and my hand on the handle. If they were waiting to grab me, at least I would have the satisfaction of scaring the pants off them by barging through the door and yelling 'RRRAAAHHHH!' I went in, heaving the door wide open. I just had time to see the two shoes in the middle of the floor, one mini, one mega, when I was grabbed from behind, bundled into the room and sat on by Bruno. He and Thurston must have taken their shoes off and tiptoed into Mum and Dad's bedroom so that they could trap me.

'What's up?' I gasped with what breath I could find.

'Look what Sniff found in your waste-paper basket,' said Thurston, holding up a wrinkled sheet of paper, criss-crossed by bits of Sellotape. It was a fair cop. I could see what it was.

'He was rootin' about in there,' said Bruno, shifting his weight a bit, to pin both my arms down with his knees. 'He was after the butterscotch left in the popcorn carton and he happened to toss *this* on to the floor.'

'Torn up, of course,' said Thurston. 'But I managed to stick it back together again. Shall I read it to you?'

'Don't bother,' I said, but he read it anyway. It was from the Boxing Board of Controls.

'Dear Mr Moore,' Thurston read. 'Thank you for your most interesting enquiry. I have to tell you, however, that we have searched our records and we can find no trace of any boxer being counted out while standing on his head. If you have any further enquiries, do not hesitate to get in touch with us again. Yours sincerely . . .'

'Well-known fact, huh?' said Bruno, flicking my ears in time with his words.

'Yeah, well what about that rice ship and jumping bean rubbish?' I wheezed.

'Thought you'd keep the letter quiet for long enough for us to forget about it, eh?' said Thurston. 'Well, you under-estimated the detective powers of Sniffo the Wonderdog.'

'The traitor,' I gasped. 'Anyway, that wasn't detective work; he was after the popcorn.'

'Sussed you out though,' said Thurston, waving the letter and dancing about with it. 'More brains than Lassie, any day, haven't you boy?' He looked round. 'Where's he gone?'

'In the garden,' I panted, twisting sideways a bit under Bruno's weight, to give myself some breathing space.

'How do you know?' said Thurston, looking under the bed.

'It's a well-known fact,' I said. 'Anyone who leaves shoes lying about in this house gets them buried in the garden by Sniffo the Wonderdog.'

'WHHHAAT?' yelled Bruno, rolling sideways off me. It was true. Sniff had left him and Thurston one shoe each.

'Better hurry up!' I called after them as they crashed down the stairs. 'He could be half way to Australia by now!'

The Taming of Sniff

'The trouble as I see it,' said Dad, through his breakfast, 'is that we have ceased to see the dog as a dog.'

Some of his breakfast caught my attention as it sailed through the air towards Mum when he said 'trouble'. I think it was an oat-flake. Mum didn't notice. She was tucking Sal's shirt into her dungarees with one hand, while peering into a book she was holding flat on the table with the other.

'I agree with you up to a point,' said Mum, who had not the faintest idea what he was going on about.

'I know what you mean, Dad,' I said, slipping a bit of bacon rind under the table where I knew it would be appreciated. 'I certainly don't think of him as a dog. I think of him as a raving loony.'

'Exactly! Proves my point,' said Dad. 'Loonies are people. We've let that dog become too human.'

When he said 'proves', another little shower of muesli sailed across the table.

All the time she was getting tucked in, Sal stood next to her high chair with her eyes fixed on the bit of Dad's breakfast that had landed first. She stretched out her arm over the edge of the table, and pressed her forefinger on it. Then she brought her forefinger close to her nose and inspected whatever it was with intense interest. When she pointed her finger under the table, Sniff's long red tongue slapped out and licked it clean.

Sal clattered out of the kitchen and Sniff followed her close in case she had anything else on her worth licking. Mum lifted her book, peered into it, put it face down, looked up at the ceiling and started muttering. She had a look of deep concentration. Her hand groped for her tea mug, missed, and she sat for quite a few seconds taking little sips at a pot of pansies.

I couldn't hear what she said but it sounded like, 'I gotta, you potty, he wanna bananary celery.' She was teaching herself Italian.

'That dog,' Dad said, his thumb pointing in the direction that Sal and Sniff had taken. 'Do you realize that under the surface even *that* dog is an intensely adaptable, intelligent, mentally and physically skilful creature?'

Mum stopped going 'wallaby hoppetty jimini rabbitty' and stared with her mouth open at Dad.

'I read about it in *The Guardian*,' Dad went on.

'There's an animal psychologist who says that at the moment dogs are functioning at the level of zombies while they have the potential to be geniuses.'

'You're the language expert, Mum,' I said. 'Can you give us a translation for all that?'

'What it means, you cheeky little ignoramus,' said Dad, playfully applying a death-grip to the back of my neck, 'is that Sniffo is not as stupid as he looks and that's official.'

'Well, if you ask me he's just a plain zombie. That's my theory,' I said.

Mum, who had been surprised out of her Italian by the amazing suggestion that Sniff had a brain, ignored my remark. 'And what do we have to do to bring out this untapped brilliance?' she asked.

'I am going to start by pointing out to him that there are more interesting things in life than eating bits off the Monopoly board.'

'That's your fault, Ben,' said Mum. 'You and Thurston and Max were playing with it last night. You should have put it away.'

'How did I know somebody was going to eat the bits? What bits exactly, anyway, Dad?'

'Only the top hat and the boot, the dice and three or four houses. He chucked them up on the patio when I let him out. You can go and collect them after breakfast and give them a wash.'

'Yuck! *Dad*! Do you mind? I've just eaten.'

'Anyhow, how do you propose to "point out to him" as you put it, that he should become a reformed doggy?' Mum wanted to know.

'A touch of animal psychology, that's all,' said Dad. He lifted his eyebrows up and down twice – which usually meant he was kidding, but you could never be sure with my dad.

*

'The main thing to remember,' said Dad, 'is that dogs are pack animals. They look to us as pack-leaders to be told how to behave. Right?'

We were standing under one of the chestnut trees at the edge of the playing field where Sniff specially liked to run about. Mostly he didn't wait to be invited out but just barged through the gap in the fence at the bottom of the garden and went where he wanted – or tunnelled under it when this way was blocked. It was a bit chilly that evening and growing dark, so Sniff was well pleased but slightly surprised to be invited out for a walk with me and Dad. There was a field of tall Brussels sprouts next to the recreation part at the top end of the playing field and Sniff had disappeared into it some time before.

'When you say "look to *us* as pack-leaders" . . . d'you mean all of us, Mum and Sal and me as well as you?'

'Ah,' said Dad, who didn't look too sure about that

one. 'Well, technically, I suppose I'm the leader of our pack, so I thought I'd undertake his redisciplining programme.'

'Did you tell Mum about this?' I asked. 'About you being the leader of the pack and everything? Or Sal? He's Sal's dog, in a way. He followed her home, remember.'

'Yes, well, don't worry about that, Ben. What I'm doing here is . . . Well, I'm just talking *technically* for the moment,' Dad said. 'I mean, as you know, Mum and I like to share the responsibility for things . . . It's not that I'm the *boss* in the old-fashioned sense of the word, it's just that, well, Sniffo's got to learn about what's what and not just go on as he always has. We can't let him go on sleeping exactly where he wants, begging at the table, running off, chasing motorbikes, eating plastic buckets and chess pieces . . .'

'And Monopoly bits,' I put in, remembering the nasty business with the Dettol and the rubber gloves I'd had to face just after breakfast.

'Exactly. So from now on we've got to be a bit firmer with him, so that the daft old batbrain knows exactly what's expected of him. Right? I'm not talking about whacking him on the nose with a rolled-up newspaper or any of that nonsense. Just firm, fair handling. That's the secret. OK? You see, psychologically speaking, he's confused. He's not sure whether to be a proper dog, doing what his pack-leader says, or some naughty little human being. So what we're going to do from here on is to unconfuse him.'

There was nobody about now, because anybody with any sense had gone home and curled up in front of a warm telly. 'So what's the plan, Dad? I hope it isn't going to take long, by the way, 'cause I'm freezing.'

'We reward the good behaviour and we reprimand him . . .'

'Tick him off?'

'Right. Reprimand him when he fails to obey a simple signal or command. We just keep it simple . . . cut out the confusion. See what I'm getting at? Now where is he?'

'In among the Brussels sprouts.'

'Where? I can't see him.'

'Hang on,' I said. I gave a whistle and Sniff popped up above the level of the towering sprouts, balancing on his back legs like an inquisitive kangaroo. He pogoed up and down on the spot for a second. Dad was really tickled by this and when Sniff disappeared from view, dropping down on to all fours again, he said, 'Cute the way he does that, isn't it? He looks like a ballet dancer. Give him another whistle.'

In hope of a repeat performance, I plugged my two little fingers under my tongue again and gave him another blast, but this time Sniff didn't stand up. Instead, he charged straight towards us. We couldn't see him at all at first, only a rapidly moving line of spray that hissed and streamed back like smoke from a funnel as he slapped and shouldered through the shadowy green plants. With twenty metres to go, he began to vault, crashing and smacking among the sprouts and sometimes leapfrogging them, until he reached us. He shook himself as if he'd just been swimming, and although Dad and I turned our backs on him and ran, we weren't quick enough to escape a shower-bath.

'Shouldn't you have said something to him then, Dad?' I asked, as Sniff scampered off and began nosing among the dead leaves under the chestnut trees, looking for something to bring us.

'About what?'

'About him going barmy and spraying sprout water all over us.'

'Bit of a problem there, son. I mean, this is just the sort of case where it's important to judge your moment very carefully. Supposing I'd got hold of him. Can you see how he'd have misinterpreted that? He'd have thought I was patting him, stroking him. You see? And that, of course, is a pleasurable thing for the Sniffter.'

'So you should never grab him and tick him off?'

'Well . . . not if he's in the middle of a game, no.'

'If you tell him off while he thinks he's playing, he gets confused. Right?' I asked.

'Right.'

'But if you *don't* get hold of him, or give him a whack, or tell him off, he thinks it's OK to do whatever it is he's doing?'

'Um . . . yes, I suppose he does.'

'Dad, this is really confusing.'

'No, no, it's really quite simple. We must just bear in mind that we've got to be positive. OK? Firm and Fair.'

At this point, Sniff had found what he was looking for. It was a soggy branch, slippery with rot. He dragged it backwards towards us, growling wildly and wagging his tail into a blur. Then he turned and bowed his front legs, said 'RRRALPH', and bobbed away, sideways and backwards. Back he sprang with a 'RRRALPH! RRRALPH!', a skip and a bob.

'Ah,' said Dad. 'Right. Now, you see that? That's his play signal.'

'OK. What do we do now?'

A sort of twinkling look came into Dad's eyes. 'Tell you what,' he said, 'I know this is really meant to be a formal training session but I can't really see the harm in chucking it for him.'

'But what about him spraying water all over us?'

'I've got it, I've got it,' said Dad. 'We'll use it as a teaching tool. Break a bit of the branch off. Chuck it into the middle of the sprouts again. Right? But this time, when he comes charging over, we wait until he gets precisely to the point where he's about to spray us and then we both say firmly . . .'

'And fairly,' I added.

'And fairly, yes. No. We say NO SNIFF! Quite fiercely, like that. NO, SNIFF!'

All of a sudden, Sniff let go of the branch and looked at Dad with sad, wet eyes.

'No. I don't mean NO now. No! NO, you stupid mutt!'

But it was too late. Sniff had already thrown himself down, rolled over on to his back and started whining miserably.

Dad tried to reason with him. 'I'm just going to

throw the thing . . . for . . . you . . . you . . . moron!'

'You're not getting through to him, Dad,' I said. 'Don't you think you ought to give him a touch of the old pack-leader stuff and just show him what you want?'

'Nice thinking, Ben,' said Dad. He bent over the slimy old branch that Sniff had found, put his foot firmly in the middle of it and heaved. He succeeded in breaking off a throwable chunk of branch and he waved it about over his head.

That was a bit more like it! It brought out a touch of the old Sniff. He was up off his back and jumping up at Dad like a big furry yoyo. Dad whanged the stick as far as he could into the middle of the sprout field and away went the Bouncy Beast like a bather pounding into the waves. The magic line of spray rose, swished in circles like a Catherine wheel, and then zigzagged in every direction as Sniff nosed after the stick. Dad and I stood absolutely still, forgetting how chilly we were, forgetting about the ordinary things like sprouts and dogs, and just admired the beauty of the show. For a minute, there was nothing on earth but the hiss of that misty unguessable line and the satisfying leathery slap of leaves. But it was only for a minute.

'OY, YOU!'

You don't go around with a dog like Sniff and not have to put up with a few OY, YOUs every now and then, so I wasn't all that surprised. But poor old Dad. It was a bit different for him. After all, he was the pack-leader.

He pointed to his middle button. 'Me?'

'Who'd ya fink I was talking to, the flaming tree? Course I'm talking ta you. What the eck d'you fink you're doing?'

The cheesed-off voice belonged to a large and cheesed-off bloke in wellies, a green mac and a flat tweed cap. He must have come up along one of the paths hidden by the chestnut trees. We hadn't seen him at all until he was practically up to us.

'We're . . . er . . . just walking,' said Dad.

'Not in my flaming Brussels you're not, mate!' He waved his stick angrily.

'We have no intention of going among your Brussels,' said Dad. 'We're keeping on the grass.'

'Well, what the heck's that?' he said, pointing with his stick at the fizzing vapour trail.

'Ah,' said Dad. 'What *is* that? Could that be the dog, Ben? In there? In among this gentleman's Brussels sprouts?'

'Is *that* where he got to? Naughty boy!' I said.

'Sniff! Here boy!' called Dad and I gave a couple of whistles. The smoke-line wavered and Sniff popped up at the end of it like a periscope. In the failing light he swayed as he peered to see what was going to be thrown for him next. He still hadn't found the chunk of broken branch. Perhaps he thought one of us had found it.

'Get him out of there!' growled the Brussels-man.

'Come on, Sniff. Here, boy! Here, boy!'

Sniff carried on wobbling and hopping on his hind legs, right where he was in the middle of the rows of sprouts.

'NO! Don't just stand there!' called Dad, desperately. 'Come over *here*.'

Sniff disappeared. We all waited. Nothing hap pened.

'I think he must have decided to lie down and roll over, Dad. When you said "NO" just now. That's what he did last time you said "No" to him.'

'NO! SNIFF! DON'T LIE DOWN, COME HERE!' Dad was getting nervous, I think.

'You just said "No" again,' I said.

So that's how Dad and I got soaked and ended up having to carry Sniff back home in the pitch dark. It took us ages to find him, and those wet plants didn't half whang against you when you went along the rows. The farmer or Sprout-man, whoever he was, stood at the edge of his field and roared and cursed and threatened to have us arrested if we ever came trepassing again.

Back in our warm kitchen, when he was towelled dry and Dad and I got out of our wet things, Sniff cheered up and chewed one of Dad's wet shoes just to show he was back to normal and there were no hard feelings.

'What happened to the psychology, then?' Mum said, grinning and heaving Sniff's jaws apart while Dad rescued his shoe. 'The pack-leader didn't get much training done, did he?'

'NO,' said Dad, firmly.

Sniff lay down and rolled over on his back.

'Cor, look at that, Dad,' I said. 'He really has learnt something!'

'So have I,' said Dad. 'You were right. He *is* a raving loony!'

Other great reads from ***Red Fox***

Other great reads from **Red Fox**

Discover the exciting and hilarious books of Hazel Townson!

THE MOVING STATUE

One windy day in the middle of his paper round, Jason Riddle is blown against the town's war memorial statue.

But the statue moves its foot! Can this be true?

ISBN 0 09 973370 6 £1.99

ONE GREEN BOTTLE

Tim Evans has invented a fantasic new board game called REDUNDO. But after he leaves it at his local toy shop it disappears! Could Mr Snyder, the wily toy shop owner have stolen the game to develop it for himself? Tim and his friend Doggo decide to take drastic action and with the help of a mysterious green bottle, plan a Reign of Terror.

ISBN 0 09 956810 1 £1.50

THE SPECKLED PANIC

When Kip buys Venger's Speckled Truthpaste instead of toothpaste, funny things start happening. But they get out of control when the headmaster eats some by mistake. What terrible truths will he tell the parents on speech day?

ISBN 0 09 935490 X £1.75

THE CHOKING PERIL

In this sequel to *The Speckled Panic*, Herbie, Kip and Arthur Venger the inventor attempt to reform Grumpton's litterbugs.

ISBN 0 09 950530 4 £1.25

Other great reads from ***Red Fox***

THE WINTER VISITOR Joan Lingard

Strangers didn't come to Nick Murray's home town in winter. And they didn't lodge at his house. But Ed Black had—and Nick Murray didn't like it.

Why had Ed come? The small Scottish seaside resort was bleak, cold and grey at that time of year. The answer, Nick begins to suspect, lies with his mother—was there some past connection between her and Ed?

ISBN 0 09 938590 2 £1.99

STRANGERS IN THE HOUSE Joan Lingard

Calum resents his mother remarrying. He doesn't want to move to a flat in Edinburgh with a new father and a thirteen-year-old stepsister. Stella, too, dreads the new marriage. Used to living alone with her father she loathes the idea of sharing their small flat.

Stella's and Calum's struggles to adapt to a new life, while trying to cope with the problems of growing up are related with great poignancy in a book which will be enjoyed by all older readers.

ISBN 0 09 955020 2 £1.95

Other great reads from **Red Fox**

Discover the great animal stories of Colin Dann

JUST NUFFIN

The Summer holidays loomed ahead with nothing to look forward to except one dreary week in a caravan with only Mum and Dad for company. Roger was sure he'd be bored.

But then Dad finds Nuffin: an abandoned puppy who's more a bundle of skin and bones than a dog. Roger's holiday is transformed and he and Nuffin are inseparable. But Dad is adamant that Nuffin must find a new home. Is there *any* way Roger can persuade him to change his mind?

ISBN 0 09 966900 5 £1.99

KING OF THE VAGABONDS

'You're very young,' Sammy's mother said, 'so heed my advice. Don't go into Quartermile Field.'

His mother and sister are happily domesticated but Sammy, the tabby cat, feels different. They are content with their lot, never wondering what lies beyond their immediate surroundings. But Sammy is burningly curious and his life seems full of mysteries. Who is his father? Where has he gone? And what is the mystery of Quartermile Field?

ISBN 0 09 957190 0 £2.50

The latest and funniest joke books are from Red Fox!

THE OZONE FRIENDLY JOKE BOOK
Kim Harris, Chris Langham, Robert Lee, Richard Turner

What's green and highly dangerous?
How do you start a row between conservationists?
What's green and can't be rubbed out?

Green jokes for green people (non-greens will be pea-green when they see how hard you're laughing), bags and bags of them (biodegradable of course).

All the jokes in this book are printed on environmentally friendly paper and every copy you buy will help GREENPEACE save our planet.

* David Bellamy with a machine gun.
* Pour oil on troubled waters.
* The Indelible hulk.

ISBN 0 09 973190 8 £1.99

THE HAUNTED HOUSE JOKE BOOK
John Hegarty

There are skeletons in the scullery . . .
Beasties in the bath . . .
There are spooks in the sitting room
And jokes to make you laugh . . .

Search your home and see if we are right. Then come back, sit down and shudder to the hauntingly funny and eerily rib-rattling jokes in this book.

ISBN 0 09 9621509 £1.99

Discover the wide range of exciting activity books from Red Fox

THE PAINT AND PRINT FUN BOOK
Steve and Megumi Biddle

Would you like to make a glittering bird? A colourful tiger? A stained-glass window? Or an old treasure map? Well, all you need are ordinary materials like vegetables, tinfoil, paper doilies, even your own fingers to make all kinds of amazing things—without too much mess.

Follow Steve and Megumi's step-by-step instructions and clear diagrams and you can make all kinds of professional designs—to hang on your wall or give to your friends.

ISBN 0 09 9644606 £2.50

CRAZY KITES Peter Eldin

This book is a terrific introduction to the art of flying kites. There are lots of easy-to-assemble, different kites to make, from the basic flat kite to the Chinese dragon and the book also gives you clear instructions on launching, flying and landing. Kite flying is fun. Help yourself to a soaring good time.

ISBN 0 09 964550 5 £2.50

Other great reads from ***Red Fox***

CRAZY PRESENTS Juliet Bawden

Would you like to make: Pebble paper weights? Green tomato chutney? Scented hand cream? Patchwork clowns? Leather ties?

By following the step-by-step instructions in this book you can make a huge variety of gifts—from rattles for the very young to footwarmers for the very old. Some cost a few pence, others a little more but all are extra special presents.

ISBN 0 09 967080 1 £2.50

CRAZY PAPER Eric Kenneway

Origami—the Japanese art of paper folding—is easy and fun to do. You can make boats that float, wriggling snakes, tumbling acrobats, jumping frogs and many more fantastic creatures.

There are easy to follow instructions and clear diagrams in this classic guide used by Japanese schoolchildren.

ISBN 0 09 951380 3 £1.95

Other great reads from ***Red Fox***

CRAZY PAINTING Juliet Bawden

There are loads of imaginative ideas and suggstions in this easy-to-follow activity book all about painting. First it teaches you the basics: how to make your own vegetable dyes, mix paints, create a fabulous marbled effect and decorate ceramics. Then the fun begins. You can design your own curtains, make zany brooches for your friends, create your own colourful wrapping paper and amaze your family with hours of painting pleasure.

ISBN 0 09 954320 6 £2.25

DRESSING UP FUN Terry Burrows

Dressing up is always fun—for a party, a play or just for a laugh! In Dressing Up Fun you'll find loads of ideas for all kinds of costumes and make-up. So whether you'd like to be a cowboy, punk or witch, superman, a princess or the Empire State Building, youll find them all in this book.

ISBN 0 09 965110 6 £2.99

Discover the exciting Lenny and Jake adventure series by Hazel Townson!

Lenny Hargreaves wants to be a magician some day, so he's always practising magic tricks. He takes this very seriously, but his friend Jake Allen tends to scoff because he knows the tricks will probably go wrong. All the same, Lenny usually manages to round off one of the exciting and amazing adventures that they keep getting involved in with a trick that solves the problem.

The books in the series are:

The Great Ice Cream Crime
ISBN 0 09 976000 2
£1.99

The Siege of Cobb Street School
ISBN 0 09 975980 2
£1.99

The Vanishing Gran
ISBN 0 09 935480 2
£1.50

Haunted Ivy
ISBN 09 941320 5
£1.99

The Crimson Crescent
ISBN 09 952110 5
£1.50

The Staggering Snowman
ISBN 0 9956820 9
£1.50

Fireworks Galore
ISBN 09 965540 3
£1.99

The Vanishing Gran
ISBN 09 935480 2
£1.50

And the latest story—

Walnut Whirl
Lenny and Jake are being followed by a stranger. Is he a spy trying to recover the microfilm in the walnut shell Lenny has discovered in his pocket? The chase overtakes a school outing to an Elizabethan mansion and there are many hilarious adventures before the truth is finally revealed.

ISBN 0 09 973380 3 £1.99